BOOKSHOP GIRL IN PARIS

Also by Chloe Coles

BOOKSHOP GIRL
LIFE'S A BEACH

CHLOE COLES

BOOKSHOP

GIRL

IN PARIS

HOT
KEY
BOOKS

First published in Great Britain in 2020 by
HOT KEY BOOKS
80–81 Wimpole St, London W1G 9RE
www.hotkeybooks.com

A CIP catalogue record for this book is available from the British Library.

ISBN: 978-1-4714-0841-0
also available as an ebook

1

Printed and bound in Great Britain by Clays Ltd, Elcograf S.p.A.

Hot Key Books is an imprint of Bonnier Books UK
www.bonnierbooks.co.uk

Note from Chloe

If you've read the first two books in this series, then you'll know how I feel about bookshops. I love them, can't get enough of them, I think books are magic! They can take you anywhere; they can pinch you from that grimy bus seat behind the lad who's nodding along to the tinny tune playing out of his phone and plop you miles away, deep into whatever world you're reading about.

In my first ever author's note I wrote about how bookshops have been a massive four-finger-Kit-Kat-sized chunk of my life. But after being a Bookshop Girl for AGES and scoffing a lifetime's supply of Kit-Kats, I'll let you into in a secret; the best thing about bookshops isn't even the books, it's the people inside the bookshops.

Obvs – yeah – there are some stinky rotten bad eggs grumbling among the shelves but there are also some of the funniest, cleverest, kindest people ever and this series is all about those ones. It turns out that Bookshop People make great friends that you'll want to keep for ever and ever.

My Bookshop Girl books have been helped along by shiny special booksellers who, like me and Paige, spend days and months and years telling people about the stories they love.

This one is all about Paige's first fling into the big wide-open world beyond Greysworth. It's about Bookshop Friends and art and living your best bohemian fantasy life. I hope that if you're stuck somewhere as grey and grotty as Greysworth, you feel like you can fling yourself into this fantasy with me and Paige, because at the very least, it's got to beat singing along to the crap that lad is playing on the bus.

Chloe x

THIS IS NOT a DRILL

'Is it too early for peanut butter brownies?' Holly asks as she looks at the clock on the staffroom wall. It's ten to nine on a Friday morning. We're fitting in a half-day shift before double Art at college this afternoon. I'm sat by the window looking out onto the high street, and I'm pretty sure I've just seen a pigeon get sucked up into one of those monster road-sweeper machines. How mad is that? One minute, you're just bobbing along the pavement, minding your own business, and the next thing you know – BAM! – you're sucked into oblivion. The bloke in the high-vis jacket looked like he knew exactly what he was doing. It's a pretty sick way to get your kicks if you ask me, but it's not enough to put me off home-made peanut butter brownies. Nothing is.

'It's never too early,' I say, watching Holly peel the lid off her mum's Tupperware box.

Adam struggles to keep the tower of paperbacks from toppling out of his locker. The kettle boils and Bruce makes a whole row of teas and coffees before passing them round. He knows exactly who has what: sugars, milk, the whole shebang.

We always have a start-up meeting before we open the shop. Usually our boss Tony tells us about how much money we made the day before. I'm not going to lie: I always zone out at that point. The figures and percentages don't mean anything to me. Maths has always made my brain feel like it's a brand-new iPhone dropped in a bubble bath. Typically I find myself staring at Tony (which hopefully makes me appear to be listening) as I imagine different hairstyles on him. My cousin had this old computer game that let you test out haircuts and colours on a webcam picture of your head instead of going to a real-life salon. Even though I've mentally tried a vast array of wild new looks on Tony, his grey Head & Shoulders, short back and sides always seem to be the best option.

Tony perches on one of the folding chairs and shuffles a big pile of *3 for 2* stickers on his lap. He says he's got an announcement to make and the room falls silent. So silent that we all hear Holly swallow the chunk of brownie she's munching in one big dry gulp.

The last time Tony walked in the staffroom with a 'special announcement' warning it was bad news. Terrible news. News that Bennett's was on its way out for good. Surely after all our hard work we can't possibly be back to square one? The new and improved shop has felt busier than it ever did before. Maybe I really *have* been zoning out when Tony's told us the figures and percentages . . . maybe we're in trouble all over again.

I dig my fingers into the yellow stuffing of my favourite armchair, as if physically holding on to the furniture in this place will keep it here.

Tony looks up from beneath his broken glasses at a room of very concerned faces. 'Oh, it's not *bad* news. Don't panic!'

'Thank God for that!' Holly sighs, stuffing another slice of gooey chocolate heaven in her mouth.

Tony smiles. 'We've got a new starter doing his induction today.'

Wow! A newbie! Nobody has joined Bennett's Books since me and Holly started here nine whole months ago. A lot can happen in nine months. Obviously human *life* can be formed in that time. Not that that's happened to anybody who works here, but that's by the by. In the nine months that I've worked in this shop my little gaggle of bookseller chums and I have managed to save this place from vanishing from Greysworth town centre, we've moved to a shiny new location on the high street, and collectively we've read *hundreds* of books.

'He'll be doing part-time weekend hours around his degree . . . His name is Blaine.'

BLAINE?!

My jaw drops. Fully DROPS like a carriage on one of those massive rides at Thorpe Park.

I can't move, or speak, or blink. Just as well Holly is doing the talking for me.

She grills our boss. 'Blaine?! Blaine Henderson? Is his name Blaine Henderson?!'

'Yes, that's him.' Tony grimaces, adjusting his glasses on the bridge of his nose.

'I don't believe it! Did he actually *apply* to work here? After everything he *did?*' Holly's spitting furious chocolate-chip crumbs.

'You can't hire him.' I shake my head. 'You do *know* he's the person who nearly destroyed our campaign to save this place?! You know he'd been *shoplifting* from our old store?!'

'Well . . .' Tony grumbles, 'it turns out that his father is on the board of directors for Bennett's. It's in our best interest to accept him for this role.' He shrugs, helpless.

'You're kidding,' I whisper in disbelief.

Adam raises his eyebrows, arms folded. 'Wow . . . I guess what they say is true: it's not *what* you know, but *who you know . . .*'

'He's even more pathetic than I'd thought. If it wasn't bad enough that he was stealing from a bookshop that was facing closure; he was stealing from a bookshop that *his dad also worked for.*' I look at Holly for answers, but she's just as stunned as I am.

'Sounds like a right spoiled brat to me.' Maxine sighs as she blows on her mug of instant coffee.

'I'm not mad keen on the idea myself,' says Tony. 'But, hey, who knows? Maybe we should give him a chance; he might not be as bad as we're all expecting him to be?'

Since when was Tony such a Good Samaritan, giving everyone the benefit of the doubt? Is this not the same manager who asked me to *remove* the picture I'd photoshopped of Adam's face onto Mariah Carey's body, with the caption All I Want for Christmas is SHRINK-WRAP ON BOOKS WITH INTRICATE DIE-CUT DUST JACKETS. Cut-throat. Heartless.

'I don't want any trouble, Paige. Please just do your best to make him feel welcome here.'

What fresh lunacy is this?! Why should *I* make him feel welcome? Why is it as if *I'm* the only one who has a problem with him? He nearly cost us our jobs. Our livelihoods. *All* of us.

I feel like that road-swept pigeon. BAM! It's not a road sweeper and a high-vis vest that's sucked me into oblivion; it's a sulky art-school boy with a leather jacket and an earring.

And he's just walked right into *my* staffroom.

'Hey, Paige. Hi, Holly.'

Turns out there is one thing in this world that can put me off peanut butter brownies.

BLAINE PAIN

I can't believe he has the audacity to come back here. After everything he did.

I seethe by a trolley of shelving as I watch Tony train Blaine on the tills. HOW can he be trusted to use the TILLS and take OTHER PEOPLE'S MONEY with his track record?! Hardly any time has passed since we all watched him leg it from the bookshop occupation protest, dripping in sprinkler-system water and SHAME.

He still looks . . . y'know, like he *did* before. Tall, dark and infuriating. I have *eyeballs*; it's not like I can't see how aesthetically pleasing he is. But it's funny how realising what a let-down he really is has changed the way I see him. It's pretty much like the day Adam read me that article about the humungous percentage of human faeces they detected on the McDonald's touchscreens. I haven't looked at a hot apple pie in the same way since.

Oh great. Blaine is shelving books in the Art department. No. Not having it. This is just too close for comfort. I clench my knuckles round the handles of the old metal shelving trolley. It's stacked high with new books. Oh, how I'd love to ram this into him. Crush him under the hardbacks and hear his puny bones snap under the wheels.

I can't take it any more. Why should I keep my mouth shut? Why shouldn't I just say exactly what we all must be thinking?

'What are you doing?' I ask him, keeping a steady eye on him in case he does a runner with the Hieronymus Bosch he's holding.

'I'm just putting some of the books on the shelves. We got a new delivery.' He blinks at me, like it's the most normal thing in the world for him to be in front of me stating the obvious.

'No, I mean, what are you doing *here*? Why are you working here after . . . *everything*? What happened to your job at Coleman's?'

Even just talking to him about Coleman's makes my stomach feel like somebody's emptied the bit of a hole punch that collects all the little punched-out holes and scattered them all over the carpet. Despite it being one of my favourite places in this town, the mecca for all art and office supplies this side of Milton Keynes, I've deliberately avoided it just so I don't have to see Blaine.

He rests an elbow on the Artist Monographs shelf and it drives me crazy to see him so at ease. So comfy! I don't *remember* doffing my Artful Dodger cap or singing 'Consider yourself at home' to him as he breezed into our staffroom!

'Oh, I was just on a temporary contract; they let me go, but my dad wants me to have a job here so . . .' He shrugs and pouts.

I feel my cheeks, my ears and my arms prickle and turn red. How can anybody feel so entitled?

'Look, Paige.' He lowers his voice to a whisper. 'I know we haven't seen each other for a while . . . Can we just start over?'

I was never going to say '*Yeah, sure, fine, no probs, water under the bridge off a duck's back, ol' buddy, ol' pal,*' but I didn't even get a chance to tell him to piss off before we were rudely interrupted by a customer asking to be shown the 'books about talking to angels'.

Eff my actual *L*.

ART ROOM WOMB SHREDDING MISERY

The drain in the Art room always smells. Really bad. Like egg sandwiches in a sweaty lunchbox. I'm sat right next to the big square sink clogged up with paintbrushes and clay sculpting tools and those plastic PVA spatula things you don't see much beyond primary school.

I slump on the desk and stare at the canvas on the wall. It's a former student's work. A portrait of a crying woman. In purple. It's a bit emo TBH. Must have been part of a Picasso-themed project because it's all jaggy and cubic. It's been nailed up above Mr Parker's desk for as long as I can remember, but I'm wondering what she's crying about for the first time today.

Maybe it's period pain. That Day One womb-shredding ache that all the hot-water bottles in the Midlands couldn't sooth. It could be that she's had her heart set on a cheese and onion bake and has trudged all the way through the town centre to Greggs to find that they only have the beef chilli ones on offer . . . Maybe *her* sworn enemy decided to turn up at *her* place of work and put in a few hours each week just to ruin her life . . . Or maybe she's crying because she too has had to sit through Mr Parker's doom and gloom monologue about how difficult it is to get into university these days. My God, it's eye-wateringly dry.

'It might seem like a long way off, but it's something you'll really need to start thinking about . . .'

Duh. I've known that I've wanted to flush out of the toilet that is Greysworth for as long as I can remember. And I've already narrowed my humungous pile of prospectuses down to a Top Three Tickets Out Of Here. But the way he is banging on about 'how competitive' it is makes it all seem so . . . *hard*.

'Universities want to see that you're *hungry* for art. They'll want to know all about the exhibitions and galleries you've been to . . .'

Hungry for art. Well, I'm definitely hungry. In fact, I'm starving. My belly is RUMBLING to get away. But where am I supposed to collect all of this stuff in Greysworth? We don't have any galleries with cutting-edge exhibitions here. There's a museum about the old shoe factory that every school in town has rinsed for trips over the years. Doubt that collection of dusty old boots is whetting anybody's appetite.

'This is the kind of thing you'll need to include in your personal statements. Just *think* of all the applications these people have to read through. The competition is *fierce*. So consider what you can say about yourself to stand out from the crowd. To impress.'

Jeeez.

As we trudge out of the school gates later and Holly tells me she's already decided what she's going to order from Nando's with Jamie tonight, I can't help but feel a bit sick about personal statements and applications and THE FUTURE.

For an art teacher Mr Parker doesn't have much *imagination*. He's suggesting that we apply for courses at less competitive unis.

'You'll be fine, Paige. Don't worry about it.'

That's easy for Holly to say; she's got her heart set on a creative writing course and has already been shortlisted for a national poetry prize that the course leader judges on. Mr Parker isn't telling *her* to apply to less competitive courses.

'Have fun at Nando's, Hol.'

She smiles. 'I'll make sure I put a little bit of Sprite in my Coke just for you!'

It's a must. If you ever have the option to pour your own fizzy drinks and you don't mix them up to create something altogether fizzier, then you're missing out. Burger King Fanta and Dr Pepper aren't a match made in heaven, but the thrill of running wild on that machine is tastier than anything I've ever known.

I guess that's not really something I can include in my application.

Please give me a place on your course. I like drawing and when I'm not avoiding my sworn enemy at work, you can find me dicking about with the drink dispenser in Pizza Hut.

How's that for a personal statement?

I power-walk along Billing Road and pass by the boys' school. It used to be the highlight of the journey home when we were younger, that posh old building, wall to wall with tall boys with long hair and guitar cases slung on their shoulders, football boots shoved into their bags. They were older than us, and dreamy. Now that I'm in sixth form it's all snotty, spotty little idiots who go there. I do my best to hurry past the gates and avoid all eye contact before some little shit calls me a lesbian.

'OI!' One of the lads pulls a can of Pepsi out of another boy's sweaty hands and starts kicking it around on the tarmac. Why are pubescent boys so horrible to each other?

I should not get emotionally invested in any of this playground drama. I've got bigger fish to fry. *Just walk, Paige, walk*.

I guess I hadn't really considered the possibility of being rejected from every uni I apply to. Mr Parker said there's a thing called *clearing* if that happens . . .

But what if I *am* a total reject? What if I'm trapped here for eternity? What if I –

OUCH!

That can of Pepsi crashes against the side of my head.

I hate today.

FRENCH EXCHANGE

Saturday morning. I trudge past the empty M&S and dodge the pools of Friday-night vomit that decorate the pavements all the way to work. Blaine is sitting on the bench outside Bennett's. Great. When he takes a drag on his cigarette his cheeks hollow out and he bats his lashes at me. His eyes glitter like the cartoon diamonds in *Snow White and the Seven Dwarfs*. I mentally PUNCH MYSELF for thinking that.

'Morning, Paige.'

Now, my initial response would be something along the lines of '*Oh, hi there, you crusty scab of a human being boy*', but I'm trying a new approach. I cannot let him get to me. Or, at least, I cannot let it be *seen* that he's getting to me. I take a deep breath.

'HiBlaine.' Said as one word. Incredibly hard to be

normal around somebody you'd much rather spit Apple Tango at.

I knock on the glass door to catch the attention of the cleaner who's dragging a Henry hoover along the birthday card display inside the shop. He can't hear me over the Ministry of Sound Club Anthems on his headphones. Blaine is up and standing next to me now. *Come on.*

I don't want to be trapped out here with him for any longer than I have to be.

Can you be 'trapped' with someone if you're out in the open air on the street?

Yes, I think you can. I defo feel like I'm *trapped* in this godforsaken town with him.

I'm pounding on the door to get into a shop that I'll be *trapped* with him in for the next seven and a half hours. No luck.

I just hate standing *around* with him like this. I feel like throwing my head into the dog-poo bin. I bang even louder. It's very dangerous to have music so loud on your headphones that you totally block out your surroundings. What if there was a fire?! This has to be some kind of violation of health and safety rules.

I put my all into banging on the door and waving my arms around so that I catch the cleaner's attention.

If I could just get inside, then I know I could avoid Blaine until it's time for us to open.

'Bloody hell, Paige! What are you doing?!' It's Tony. 'I've never seen you so eager to start a shift!' This isn't the first time he's looked at me like I'm insane. I can almost guarantee it will not be the last.

Tony scuttles into his office. It's just me and Blaine in the staffroom.

Silence. I plonk myself on the chair by the window and bury my face in a book.

'What are you reading?' He's talking to me. Interrupting me.

'*The Woman Destroyed.*' It's by Simone de Beauvoir. I bought it because I liked the cover, and I read her most famous book *The Second Sex* as part of my resolution to work my way through everything we have in our Women's Studies section. I actually bought this particular book in a charity shop because even though I have all the books I could ever want and need right at my fingertips as a Bennett's Bookshop Girl, it's actually *nowhere near* all the books I could ever want and need. I love charity book shopping. I love the yellowed pages, the *Merry Christmas, Darlings* written on the inside of the covers. I cannot and will not resist that feeling you get when you find a book

17

and hold it in your hands and know that you must have it, and I don't really care about where I'm standing when that happens to me.

I don't say any of this to Blaine. I just shrug when he says 'Oh. Cool.'

Back to Simone. It's just me and her. Nobody else in the world, let alone in this room –

'What's this?' He hunches and runs his fingers along my handwritten words that are on a microwave-ready-meal-splattered piece of paper taped to the fridge: PETITION TO GET A TOASTER IN THE STAFFROOM.

I thought it was pretty self-explanatory really. Unless he can't read, in which case he really isn't qualified to be here at all. Somebody should strip him of that Bennett's lanyard at once.

I close my *Woman Destroyed* and begin, 'It was a petition I started a few weeks ago . . .'

I mean, just *think* of the delicious opportunities . . . Crumpets and breakfast muffins and those sugary waffles that come in little individually wrapped packets. And obviously – TOAST. It would really transform a rainy-day lunch break. I could eat a whole loaf of white bread if it was toasted and slathered in melty butter.

'Everybody signed it . . . as you can see, but Tony shut

it down when he said they used to have one, but it played havoc with the smoke detectors.'

He blinks at me. 'You never stop, do you?'

Excuse me?

I don't know what I'm supposed to say to that. What does he mean by that?

I 'never stop'. *I never stop wishing he would hand in his notice and LEAVE.*

Voices in the corridor. Other human life! Thank GOD!

'I got up early and watched all seven episodes this morning before work.' Holly swings the door open, mid-convo with Bruce who's hanging his anorak on a peg as they discuss some Netflix documentary about a serial killer in America.

Bruce kicks his 'work shoes' on, which are basically a glorified slipper. I respect him for this. We're on our feet all day; comfort is important. I guess I'd wear slippers to work, but, seeing as the ones I have at home are big squashy Hello Kitties that are all grey and manky from taking the bins out in the rain, I don't think I'd get away with it somehow.

'Morning, Paige!' Holly blows a kiss and I catch it. 'Hi, Blaine.'

She can't help but grimace at me after saying that,

because YES IT IS AWKWARD. WHY IS HE HERE?

While Holly tells me all about her hot (lemon and herb) date at Nando's, the rest of the Bennett's crowd arrive and I can almost pretend that Blaine Henderson doesn't exist at all.

'Right then.' Tony rolls up his cable-knit sleeves and leans on the kitchenette counter. It's that time of day. Sales figures and imaginary makeovers! 'Good morning, everybody!'

Good morning. Wow. *Somebody* got out on the right side of bed this morning. Tony doesn't usually say 'good morning'. He doesn't usually say 'good' to be honest. Maybe it's his birthday or something.

'We were down on target yesterday, but not *down-down*, just the usual down.'

Or maybe he's won the lottery.

'It should be fairly busy today, so I reckon we'll hit our targets if we're lucky.'

That must be it: he's an instant millionaire. Managing Bennett's is just a hobby for him now. He'd be just the sort of person to become filthy rich and shock us all by turning up to work every day 'because he'd miss it otherwise', despite years of having us all fooled into thinking he's the most miserable man alive.

'I've got some exciting news!' He licks his barely there lips.

Well, this doesn't sound like his usual THE END IS NIGH routine. He actually looks pleased. It's an unusual look on Tony, I must say. I haven't seen him this excited since he pointed out that we couldn't accept gift vouchers from competing bookshops to a disappointed customer who had got her cards mixed up in her purse.

'Some of you may be familiar with one of France's most famous bookshops . . . Pages of Paris?'

OMG, yes! I raise my hand, like an absolute loser, while my colleagues nod their heads. (*Because we're in an adult work environment, not school, Paige, you freak.*)

'*What's Pages of Paris?!*' Holly hisses at me.

'*I showed you their Instagram, remember?*' I whisper back.

I show Holly A LOT of things on Instagram to be fair, so it's understandable that she still looks baffled. I can see her mind flicker with all the pics of teacup pigs, retro interiors and flouncy vintage gowns I've pinged her way. Pages of Paris looks like bookshop HEAVEN, though! It was facing closure after decades of being an iconic English-language bookshop. The owner, Margot Redford, died with no relatives and nobody to pass her beloved business on to. The people of Paris were heartbroken.

So a group of dedicated booklovers set up a co-op to keep the old shop going. There's no manager, no owner, just people who love the place sharing the task of keeping it running. And rather than just keeping it running, it looks like the place is *thriving*. Buzzing with workshops and celeb appearances, they've even added a coffee shop where every drink is named after a literary legend. It looks like a dreamy, dreamy paradise.

'I received an email last night from the team at Pages of Paris, who have heard all about our recent fight to keep Bennett's open. As an act of kindness and solidarity they've invited us to take part in a bookshop exchange! Two members of staff will have the chance to spend a week in Paris, while we'll welcome two French booksellers here to Greysworth!'

WOW. I grab Holly's arm. How amazing! This would be an actual dream come true.

Just THINK of all the arty-farty-culture we'd get to soak up! I can see it now: we'd spend the day working at Pages of Paris . . . wander along to the Louvre . . . say *bonjour* to the *Mona Lisa* . . . and eat ALL the bread and pastries and cheese we could get our French-manicured hands on. That would certainly give Mr Parker and those university admissions people something to read about in my personal statement. I'd have the chance to see and do and taste things I've only read about in French GCSE textbooks or watched on *The Aristocats*.

There was a French exchange at school back in Year Eight. Even though French is one of my fave subjects (after Art and English Lit, but waaaaaay way above Maths, Science and RE). (And OMG miles above PE, but I didn't even count that initially because how is PE even a subject? It's just two hours of trainer-related cruelty a week, so really this isn't at all relevant. I get mad at the mere *thought* of PE.) I was way too shy to stay with a family of strangers when all I could say with confidence was '*Où est la piscine?*' The French kids that came to our school were cool and sporty or cool and gothy, and listened to strange techno music we'd never heard of. When our girls came back to school they told us that they mainly ate weird quiche, but got to smoke and drink and ride on the backs of French-boy mopeds.

So maybe I missed out on a world of fun back then, but this is NOW. There's never been a better time for me to fling myself out into the world. I mean, come ON. Pages of Paris. It practically has my name written all over it!

'So how will we decide who goes to Paris?' Adam asks.

'Well, let's see a show of hands.' (Okay, so maybe

sometimes it is permitted in an adult work environment. Noted.) 'Who would like to go to Paris?' Tony throws his own arm up as he speaks.

Everybody. Of course everybody wants to swap Greysworth for Paris. There's no comparison, is there?

Holly winks at me. Yes-yes-yes!

'Names in a hat?' Nikki suggests.

'Names in a hat.' Tony nods. 'We'll do it this afternoon if we get a quiet moment, but for now we should open up. Let's get the cash and start the day . . . *Merci*, everybody!'

As I open the little plastic bags of pound coins and drop them into the till drawer, Adam asks the most important question of the day. 'Right? I'm taking requests.' He's turning the dusty old CD player on at the plug. 'What do you want to listen to?'

'Something French!' I suggest. 'To get us in the mood for the exchange!'

'I wouldn't mind my name being pulled out!' Adam rubs his hands together with glee. 'Think of all the *fromage*! It's not every day you get to skip over the Channel on a bookseller's wage, is it? It would be a great opportunity . . .'

Maxine smiles. 'Oh, you'd absolutely love it there, Paige.'

'Wow, really, Maxine? Have you been?'

'Oh yeah. Years ago . . . with an old boyfriend.' She runs her fingers through her grey hair and laughs. 'Pages of Paris was the best part. The rest of that weekend was bloody awful!'

I want to know all the gory deets about Maxine's historic holiday from hell, but, alas, our first customer of the day waves to get my attention and shouts, 'Books on IBS. Where are they?'

Good morning, Greysworth.

THE YES/NO RUBBER OF DESTINY

Right, I'm two and a half hours into my shift and have already pored over every guidebook we have on Paris in the Travel section. I pretended to be tidying. I don't think anyone has noticed that it's still a mess over in that corner and that, in fact, I've done zero tidying.

Uh-oh, I think I've baited myself out by struggling to fold this street map back up. Cover blown. The 18th arrondissement is all up in my face and Blaine is walking towards me. What's French for 'get lost'?

'I see you,' he says, watching me scrunch the city of Paris flat. 'Looking at the guidebooks.'

'Yeah.' It's actually one of my favourite things to do on a rainy-day shift. Just dive into the travel books and imagine I'm somewhere warm and beautiful like the Seychelles or Barbados. Palm trees and sea that surely can't actually be that blue in real life. When the air conditioning packed in during the heatwave a few months ago, I cooled down by flicking through the Lonely Planet guide to Iceland. That's the magic of books, isn't it? That you can lose yourself in the possibility of Northern Lights and luxury igloos when the reality of your surroundings might be more frozen-peas-from-Iceland. This isn't something I'd expect Blaine to understand.

'So you're pretty keen on going to Paris?' He does this thing where he nods and pouts, like he's bored by everything that ever existed.

'Well, yes. I'd love to go. I've always wanted to go.'

'Have you never been?'

'No.' I feel my cheeks burn. They tingle with the shame that I've never had the chance. 'Have you?'

'Yeah, a bunch of times.' He shrugs. 'It's all right.'

'Excuse me, sir? Would you direct me to your books on military history?'

Some bloke in a wax Barbour jacket goes straight to Blaine to ask that question, even though I'm stood *right here*. I hate it when men do that. Ask the male member of staff like he'd have all the answers just because he's got a few hairs on his chest.

'IT'S UPSTAIRS.' I shout it over the conversation, because I won't stand for it.

The old codger stares at me, mouth agape, like he doesn't understand what I've just said. So I clarify.

'The books about men shooting other men *with weapons made by women* are all upstairs on the first floor.' I smile. 'My colleague Blaine can show you to them if you like.'

Off they go.

I slouch on the wheelie chair behind the till and bounce up and down by adjusting the height. Of course Blaine's been to Paris a bunch of times. If your dad is one of the head honchos of a big nationwide company like Bennett's, and you nick books rather than spending any money on them, well, you probably have cash to burn on baguettes and Brie.

Without even meaning to I've picked up the Rubber of Destiny from behind one of the computer keyboards. It's one of those white Staedtler erasers. The kind that would have started out as a solid rectangle but has been broken and squashed and discoloured at the edges.

A while back some long-lost anonymous Bennett's employee wrote YES on one side and NO on the other. We use it to determine all sorts of possibilities. Like the time we flipped it and it confirmed that, yes, Tony does officially hate me. It's not as if I'd need the Rubber of Destiny to tell me that, but I guess if anything it just proves its powers are legit.

It's important to hold it really tightly in your fist and concentrate on your question before tossing it.

Will I get into uni? FLIP. No.

Will I get to go to Paris? FLIP. No.

Will Blaine Henderson bugger off out of my life any time soon? FLIP. NO.

Ugh! This Rubber of Destiny SUCKS.

I chuck it away from me in disgust. It bounces and pings onto Tony's Hush Puppies as he walks past the desk.

Great.

If I ever doubted the power of the rubber, flinging it at Tony will certainly count towards his hatred for me. The rubber is right about everything, isn't it?

'Well, instead of flinging stationery at your manager, perhaps you could make yourself *useful*, Paige.'

Crap.

'We'll be drawing the name for the shop exchange soon, so we need a hat.'

I don't know how to tell him that I don't really *do* hats. Believe me, I've tried, but I think my hair's too big for it to ever work. And you need a fair amount of forehead to wear a hat, don't you? Sorry, Tony: too much hair, not enough forehead. I'm out.

'Also, what have I told you about sitting on the chair?'

Apparently it's reserved for staff with doctors' notes saying they *need* a chair. I don't think it takes a medical professional to point out that having a chair to recover from the stupidity of certain members of the public is a human right.

Holly saves me, wheeling an empty trolley she's dutifully cleared of shelving. 'I have an idea! We should use a beret for the draw! Does anyone have a beret?'

I mean, sure, Hol, it's a nice idea. 'When have you ever seen a person wear a beret in this town?!' I say.

'Have a look in lost property, Paige.'

Oh God. Tony's orders. Here I go.

Going through the lost property box by the staffroom is a fate worse than death. There's all sorts of discarded crap in here. Four umbrellas. A pair of bifocal glasses. A Boots bag containing some hay-fever nasal spray. A glove. Two scarves. One cuddly toy. And here come the hats. An old-man-slash-farmer's flat cap and a knitted hat with a raggedy pompom on top. This will have to do. An old manky green bobble hat is about as chic as Greysworth is ever going to get.

'You're my only hope, green bobble. Bring me luck. Bring me Paris!'

I clear a space on the coffee table. Let's do this. I write down the names of everyone who works here. Eight of us in total. Snip them into little strips. I think these are left-handed scissors; I'm usually much neater than this. I line all the names up on the table, then fold them each in half and sprinkle them into the green bobble one by one. I wonder if it's better for mine and Holly's names to go in first or to be nearer the top? I do a practice shake of the hat. Hard to tell. Now Blaine. It's not really *fair* for him to be entered into the draw. He's been to Paris 'a bunch of times' already, and he doesn't really deserve to go this time, does he?

Then I have an idea. It's a terrible, Grinch-y idea. An idea I'll probably never tell anyone about.

There are only two places on this trip . . . and what if me and Holly aren't picked? We'll be gutted.

Probability and maths and statistics have never been my strong point . . . but it couldn't hurt to put our names in the draw a few more times . . . just for luck. It's not like anyone will notice once all the little pieces of paper are folded up inside the hat . . .

I hold my breath and scrawl *Paige – Holly – Paige – Holly*

– *Paige* – *Holly* a few more times before shoving them into the hat.

Nikki bustles into the staffroom with armfuls of orange Sainsbury's carrier bags. 'Hello, Paige!'

As she unloads her shopping, and avocado, teabags and some green-top milk for the fridge, I pull Blaine's name out of the hat. I don't want her to see me do it, because it's a Bad Thing To Do, but it's also the best thing I've ever done.

This is a just cause. A noble cause.

Nikki holds up a bag of croissants and *pains au chocolat*. 'I bought these for the big Paris draw! Will you give me a hand?'

THE BERET OF DESPAIR

'Right then, without any further ado, let's see who'll be jet-setting off to Paris . . .'

Adam plays a famous French song by Edith Piaf: 'Non, Je Ne Regrette Rien'.

We've listened to this at school before. We had to translate the lyrics. It's basically a big banger of an anthem about having no regrets, none whatsoever.

Holly links arms with me as we all stand around and watch eagerly.

'Here we go!' Tony pulls the first piece of paper out and holds it up to read.

'Drumroll!' Holly calls out before Adam complains that she's too close to his ear and may trigger his tinnitus.

'Right, okay, well, right . . .' Tony's eyes dart around the room and he clears his throat awkwardly. 'So the first

33

name I have here is *Blaine*.'

OH GOD. NO!

Tony looks gutted. He's got a smile plastered on his face, but something in the way he's gritting his teeth tells me he thinks it's Sod's Law that after years of working for Bennett's, where the glammest place they've ever sent him has been the Marriott Hotel in Peterborough, some new kid comes along and wins a trip to Paris on his first day.

'Sweet, thanks mate.' Blaine's lips curl into a smile and he pushes his hands into his jeans pockets.

'So who's next?' Tony grumbles.

I can't watch. This is too awful. I bury my face in Holly's shoulder.

Edith Piaf rings in my ears. *No, I don't regret anything; no, I regret nothing.*

I DO, EDITH! I regret putting my name in the hat four times! I really regret my STUPID attempt at increasing my chances now.

Tony shuts his eyes and his tongue juts out in concentration.

Moment of truth.

'Paige.' I hear my name, but I can't bear to open my eyes.

'The second lucky person is Paige. Paige! Paige and Blaine, you'll be going to Paris.'

I lock myself in the staff toilet cubicle and delve into the pocket of my skirt. What piece of paper did I snatch out of the draw instead of Blaine's? Whose chances did I dash? This is awful. Bad-bad-bad. I'm a terrible person.

I unfold the paper, hands shaking.

Paige.

It's just my own dumb name in my own dumb handwriting. Okay, well, at least I didn't completely screw someone else over. This is karma, though. Karma hasn't just come back to bite me in the bum; it's having an all-you-can-eat Pizza Hut buffet with a birthday balloon tied to the back of its chair.

Maybe there's a way out of it.

Holly's better at French than I am. She got a higher mark on her oral exam. I just picked it because I like putting on accents and voices. It seemed like I could basically get a whole A level just for doing impressions. But when it comes to actually talking to a French person in France . . . it'll all just go *vamoose*, out of my head. Wait, is vamoose actually a French word?

Help. I slide down the cubicle wall. There's no way I can go through with this.

I rack my brain, willing for a way – there's got to be

a way – to get out of this, before realising I've been leaning on the sanitary towel bin this whole time.

Gross.

DUKE OF FART

'That's great news, Paige! Well done!'

Mum wouldn't be congratulating me if she knew I'd cheated.

'It's not really anything I've *done well* . . .'

'It's the luck of the draw! Hey, I hope this means you're on a winning streak . . . If it rubs off on me, maybe my lottery numbers will come up!' She squeezes me and I wince with stupid-girl guilt.

Mum said that the first and third time I got bird pooed on. And we're still not rich. Still no jackpot joy for us. This is just my luck. My first big break out of here and I'm stuck with you-know-who.

'I have to go. Just think of the personal statement.'

'Well, yeah – and the fun.' Mum doesn't say '*duuuuh*' but she may as well.

'It might not exactly be *fun*. Not with *him there*.'

She looks at me from behind her mug of tea. 'Paris is huge, Paige. You're not going to be attached at the hip with Blaine, are you? Not unless you want to be . . .' She wiggles her eyebrows mischievously.

'Mum!' I'm fuming. 'Stop it! No, I do not. No way.'

'Wow . . . I'd have loved to go to Paris when I was your age . . . In fact, I'd love to go now. Look, if you're not up for it, then I'll take your place. I don't mind travelling there and back with that Blake or whatever his name is. I'll give him a piece of my mind. Ha! He'd never want to come back to Greysworth.' She laughs.

'Well, you can't blame anyone for that.' I sigh.

'There are SO MANY things you're good at, Paige. Try not to let this personal statement business get to you.'

'I *knew* I should have done that Duke of Edinburgh thing,' I whinge.

She gasps in disbelief. 'You have got to be kidding me, Paige.'

'Well, all the teachers *said* it would look good on our uni applications, but, *oh no*, I was too good for it then, wasn't I? Thought I had more important things to do.' I shake my head at my own foolishness.

'Orienteering. Climbing up big hills in those minging

walking boots. Spending time with teachers outside of school *out of choice*. All in the name of that old Duke of Fart!' She laughs. 'You did have bigger fish to fry, and you do now! So stop moaning and brush up on your French lingo!'

BON VOYAGE!

I know, what was I thinking? I can't let one person make me want to pull a sickie on this huge, twinkling opportunity. I'll just avoid him. Paris is way bigger than Greysworth. I won't have to have anything to do with him once we're there.

Mum took the morning off work (an occasion usually saved for trips with my little brother to the orthodontist) to drop me at the station.

'Make sure you've got everything . . .' She watches as I pat myself down. Phone, tickets, passport, purse.

'Love you, Mum.' I lean over to hug her in the driver's seat.

'Uh-uh! I think you're supposed to say *Je t'aime!*'

I wriggle out of the car and haul my suitcase onto the kerb. 'Bye! *Au revoir, Maman!*'

'*Bon voyage!* Text me when you get there!' she calls out

of the car before rolling the window back up and driving towards the exit of the short-stay.

I take a deep breath. This is the first time in my life that I, Paige Turner, have been totally by myself, solo, alone, outside Greysworth. I look up at the gloomy London sky, listen to the sirens in the distance, and watch red buses plastered with West End shows and blockbusters whizz past me in a blur. I love it.

My phone buzzes. It's Holly.

We decided to send each other postcards while I'm away, because how cute are postcards?! But obviously international post cannot keep up with how regularly we'll need to send updates so we said we'd cheat by writing physical postcards and sending pics of them back and forth. It looks like she's already started. I have to zoom in to the pic to read her handwriting.

BON VOYAGE, MON AMI! I know that technically this isn't actually a postcard; it's one of those mini school photos with 'PROOF' slapped across my Year Four face, because a) I don't actually have any postcards in my room but I woke up BORED because I knew you were leaving the country today and b) this way you won't forget what I look like while you're away. Although, thank God,

I don't still have that frizz-bomb hair. Have a *magnifique* time in Paris! The world isn't ready for Paige Turner! Love from H xxxx

I'm so excited that I cackle hysterically at her school photo message before remembering I'm not in Greysworth any more. I'm outside. I'm an independent grown woman in the city, with my own passport. I send Holly a picture of St Pancras International.

See you on the other side, *bébé*! X

I glide into the station with the new case I bought from the market. I treated myself to one of those pull-along ones so I can feel like a chic jet-setter. A glamorous flight attendant from the olden days before budget airlines made people wear ugly orange or yellow uniforms.

I pat myself down again as I walk. I reckon this is a must when travelling alone. Continuous patting will not only ensure that you still have your phone, tickets, passport and purse, but it will also make you look a bit mad and hopefully deter any kind of unwanted attention from somebody madder than you.

I feel for the euros Mum gave me the other day. When

I got home from school the money was on my bed in the little paper envelope from the Post Office. I held the notes up to the light, marvelling at their foreign designs like they were a wad of Willy Wonka Golden Tickets. 'Mum, thank you! You didn't have to; I just got paid last week.'

'Well, it's not much, but it'll save you having to get any money exchanged. And you'll still take your bank card with you, won't you?'

'Yeah.' I look at the kid wearing the snorkel and armbands on the envelope. Nothing says holiday like a pair of rubber armbands. Just the sight of them makes me remember the way they'd pinch and rub uncomfortably. Probably one of the reasons I've been put off swimming for life.

'Keep it safe! That's the bread fund!'

It feels very special to be given Mum Money. Some of my friends just ask their mums for cash like it's nothing, but I've never wanted to do that. I didn't feel like I could when she'd lost her job and was struggling to find a new one. One of the best and luckiest things about working at Bennett's (other than having all the books right there) is having money. *Financial independence*. Sure, a big chunk of what I earn goes on must-read things I find at work, but I started there with the intention of saving up for uni . . .

I spent so many months collecting prospectuses and getting really excited about studying and moving away and starting my LIFE – I felt like I knew what I was doing – but since I've got caught up in this stupid personal statement . . . just thinking about it makes my chest feel tight.

I join the Eurostar security gate queue in one fluid wheelie motion.

'Hey, Paige!'

Groan.

It's Blaine.

I don't know how I'm going to glide my way out of this one.

A ROMANTIC
BREAK FOR TWO

I plonk myself in the window seat and plug my earphones into my ears immediately. I stare out of the glass and gaze over at the platform as I sense Blaine coming along the aisle towards me. Ugh, I thought I'd lost him at passport control. I think he's talking to me but I can't hear. He reaches up to shove his massive bag onto the shelf rack above my head and when he does his T-shirt rides up exposing bare naked flesh: pale soft skin and a trail of dark hair that runs down to the belt on his jeans. Oh GOD, I'm the worst. I don't get travel sickness; I just make myself sick looking at Blaine.

He sits next to me and does that thing that all boys do. When they bounce their knee frantically. Pent-up boy energy. Sit still for God's sake. It's not hard. I'm not a fidget. It's just not in my nature. I could lie perfectly still for eternity (if I had food and books within arm's reach obviously).

There's an advert by the carriage door. It says WIN A ROMANTIC BREAK FOR TWO! in big loopy writing. The picture shows a handsome couple with shiny hair and heads full of big white teeth falling about laughing in front of the Eiffel Tower. That's Paris. That's what everybody thinks about people who go to Paris and that image couldn't be further from the hellish reality I'm living right now.

Blaine twists his body towards me.

'What?' I pull my earphones out of my ears, holding them just millimetres away from my face, ready to replace his dumb voice ASAP.

'What are you listening to?'

'It's a playlist that Holly made me. A Parisian soundtrack. All French stuff, y'know.' Breathy, lashy sixties babes and jangly guitars. It's *perfect*. That girl is a genius. My fave track so far is called 'Bonnie and Clyde' because when Brigitte Bardot sings it sounds like she's saying '*Bunny* and Clyde' and if doing impressions of that was all I needed to get by in Paris, I think I'd be all right.

He nods and looks at me, like *too hard*. It makes me look away.

'What about you? What are you listening to?' He has

one earphone in, and one dangling round the collar of his leather jacket.

'Oh, you've probably never heard of them.'

UGH!

I *hate* the assumption that girls don't know anything near as much about music as boys do. A huge part of me wants to say *Oh yeah? Try me*, because I bet I *have* heard of whatever trash he's listening to, but an even bigger part of me thinks he's just an arrogant knob and I couldn't actually care less about what flows into that pierced ear of his.

Just as I'm having Serious Words with my former self for ever fancying this loser, he jumps up to get something out of his bag. We're inside the tunnel now, which means there's nothing to pretend to look at through the window, so I fake-yawn and close my eyes to give the impression that I'm sleeping. (As if I'd *ever* feel like snuggling up and snoozing next to him.)

I can sense him fiddling around with something over in his seat. I squint sideways.

No. Don't look, Paige.

I'm not looking. I'm not encouraging him.

But it's like he's trying to prise something out of a case. He's having difficulty. It's like watching (but not watching) a caveman work out how to use Deliveroo on a smartphone.

I concentrate on my award-winning fake sleep when he ELBOWS ME IN THE ARM.

'Oi! Watch it!' Totally wasn't ever asleep, was I?

'Sorry! I'm sorry! I was just trying to get this lens out of the case. I think it's stuck. I didn't mean to –'

'What is it?'

'Camera. I've bought loads of film for it.'

It looks old and fancy, but not like the massive SLR they have at school to take really embarrassing pics of assembly. The kind you'd never, ever want to see again in your life because you're dressed up as a character from *An Inspector Calls* and you'd appreciate it if it could be *removed* from the noticeboard in the English block; it *was* three years ago, after all. Something like that.

He points and shoots the camera right at me. In my face. I mean, we're sitting right next to each other. I'm no Annie Liebovitz but I know it's way too close to get a decent picture.

'Hey!' I frown, and it clicks and, oh God, it's not like it's a phone so I can demand to see how awful that pic is bound to be and DELETE IT. He is so annoying.

I shove my earphones back into my ears and text Holly.

Excusez-moi, what's the French word for DICKHEAD?

PARIS SYNDROME

I kind of wish he'd just make his own way to the bookshop. It's a bit distracting walking along the streets with him. I'm well aware that we happen to be a boy and a girl in the City of Love. Somehow, somewhere along the way, one of the wheels on my brand-new suitcase decided to give up on life, so I can't really whizz it behind me in the effortlessly cool way I'd imagined. I'm having to lug it along by my side and it's really heavy. I caught my reflection in a painted bistro window and I looked a lot like Quasimodo dragging a suitcase of Primark's finest up the steps of Notre-Dame.

Blaine actually offered to help me at one point, but I snapped at him. I don't need a *boy* to help me with my luggage. I'd rather be mistaken for literature's fave bell-ringer than give him the satisfaction of thinking I rely on him in any shape or form.

Instead I'm doing my best to take it all in. Soak up every drop of Paris. The sun is shining and we're winding through the city.

'Have you ever heard of Paris syndrome?' Blaine asks.

'Um . . . I don't think so?' I definitely haven't.

'Well, it's this condition that some people suffer from when they visit Paris for the first time and are devastated that it's not what they thought it would be like.'

I nod. A disappointing holiday can leave you devo'd, sure.

He's still talking. There's more. 'It can be, like, really extreme, though. I read something about how badly it has affected some tourists, who've travelled all the way across the world with these romantic ideas about this place being some kind of Disneyland with non-stop éclairs and cancan dancers, and then when they get here and in real life it's ugly and dirty, they have an actual physical and emotional breakdown.'

'Whoa.' I know how it feels to have something (OR A CERTAIN SOMEONE) let you down. I think it's safe to say I suffered from a mild case of Blaine Henderson syndrome last summer, but I don't believe that Paris could ever disappoint me. Bring on the fictional cancan dancing éclairs! Bring on the grot! After a lifetime in the cesspit we've come to know and love as Greysworth, where an empty branch of Sports Direct is one of the main landmarks, I'm so ready for Paris in all its grime and glory.

'That's what I like about Paris. The ugly, dirty side to the city.' He holds up his camera. 'And that's just what this baby's for.'

Oh God, gimme a break. I just rolled my eyes so hard I think I've gone blind.

If he's looking to take pics of ugly, dirty Paris, then he should just take a selfie and get over it.

I wiggle my phone out of my jacket pocket. Google Maps is frozen. The arrow telling us which direction we're facing isn't moving, even though I'm pacing around. UGH! Great.

'Blaine. I don't know where we are, do you?'

He exhales and looks around. I see his face change when he notices the old ornate wooden shutters on a building across the street. He points and shoots. Of course.

Sure, it's picture-perfect beautiful Parisian architecture, but we have a bookshop to find!

'I just don't want to get into trouble for being late for our first day . . .' I say, panicking.

He stops and smirks at me. 'Trouble? Ha! Paige, who are we going to get into trouble with?'

Something in the way he says it feels like an annoying

kid you don't know leaning behind you on the big slide in the park and telling you to hurry up when you know it's a way bigger drop than you'd expected and the possibility of getting lodged and stuck halfway down is very real. Those little sods were in every playground, pushing kids off slides and spinning roundabouts too hard and too fast. I guess they all grow up to be the Blaine Hendersons of the world.

'You told me about it yourself, Paige – it's a co-operative.'

'Yeah?'

'So there's no manager.'

It's great. I love that idea. A Tony-free, *why-are-you-late-again*-free existence appeals to every part of me. But –

'Well, the whole point of a co-operative is that the responsibility is shared by everyone who volunteers, so if we're going to take part in this exchange at all, we should at least show up.'

I give myself an imaginary pat on the back for that. Yeah, you tell him, Paige.

Oh, I know. I packed a guidebook and I think that it had a map tucked in at the back.

I try to do it with subtlety. I don't want to look like a dumb tourist rummaging through my case on the streets of

Paris. So I unzip my case ever so slightly on the pavement and stick my arm inside. Root around to find the book without exposing the full contents of my luggage to Blaine who's stood watching me while rolling a cigarette. My tongue juts out in concentration. Holly used to want to be a vet when we were younger. I think she thought it would all be dabbing kittens with fluffy bits of cotton wool and wrapping bandages round sausage dogs, until we saw a programme where a vet had to basically shove his whole arm up a pregnant cow's bum. That put her right off. If Holly could see me now, losing my limbs to this suitcase, she'd have something to say about it. Obvs this is less traumatic, despite the looks I'm getting from the locals.

Yes! Gotcha! I retrieve the guidebook. I only bought it the other week, but have scoured the descriptions of every must-see destination in Paris. It's rammed with Post-it notes and printouts and I used my special kawaii highlighters for things I really don't want to miss.

I yank the zip on my case and it breaks. I don't know how I managed that but I can't pull it closed! Now it's gaping open, innards spilling out onto the pavement.

Zips are a lifelong source of humiliation. Why, in this day and age, haven't scientists developed some kind of fastening that won't betray you like a zip? You can never fully trust a zip. I found that out the hard way when I got stuck in my Puffa jacket in Year Three. It took two dinner ladies to wriggle me and my half-eaten Babybel out of it.

Now this. Thanks a lot. What a waste of money this case turned out to be! That's the last time I'm spending my hard-earned cash on anything from Barry's Luxury Travel Accessories.

Oh GOD, no.

There's a huge tarantula-like tangle of black M&S tights flopping onto the street, and I cringe, trying to stuff it back inside before any more passers-by are haunted by the sight of the grey bobbly gusset on display.

How dare I even *think* of the word 'gusset' to myself here in Paris? It's so unglamorous.

My knickers. Out for all to see. A lacy bra, which I mentally label as 'The Sexy Bra', looks SO minging in daylight. It's about as sexy as Tony modelling the contents of the lost-property box at work. Wow. That really is shudder-worthy. There's something fundamentally wrong with my brain for even coming up with that image.

I may as well climb to the top of the Eiffel Tower and strap my billowing pair of period pants up there so they can flap around in the breeze like the tricolour flag. Just to make sure that all of Paris gets a good look, because so far as I'm concerned I've only reached about ninety per cent of the population.

Plus, to top it all off, I look like a major slob. Instead of folding my clothes neatly before packing, I spent A LOT of time watching YouTube videos of crazy professional folding techniques. Like the one about the lady in Japan who folds T-shirts into perfectly neat little parcels with one swift hand movement. It's mesmerising. After I'd wasted hours watching an entire playlist of these videos I realised how late it was and I just ended up chucking all my clothes in the case without folding a single item.

Blaine sniggers behind his cigarette. I guess it *is* kind of funny, and it's just as well he's not offering help this time. I don't need it. I've tied a jumper round the case, knotting the sleeves together to keep everything closed inside. It looks like a ghost is hugging it shut.

'Well, let's go then.' I try to say it like nothing happened. Show's over.

I'm struggling to find exactly where we are on my map. The city plan is cute and illustrated with things like cafes and art galleries enlarged so you can sort of make out where they are, but it seems like there are huge chunks of streets that aren't even included . . . I have no idea where we are.

In fact, I think we're actually LOST.

Blaine isn't bothered. Considering he's been here A BUNCH OF TIMES, he doesn't seem to know his way around. He's happily snapping away on his camera. Bending his gangly legs, jumping on and off kerbs, taking photos of street signs and puddles and graffiti. It's mildly irritating, but at least he's not pointing that thing at me any more. It would be great if he could focus some of that energy into working out where we're supposed to be going, though . . .

We wander further into what I realise is the red-light district. 'Wow! It's the Moulin Rouge!' I recognise the big neon windmill from the film. It gives me a real unexpected pang of homesickness. I just think about how cosy I was the night I watched the film on telly with Mum and Holly. Roaming the streets of Paris with this absolute moron feels a million miles away from that. I hum one of the songs from the soundtrack to myself, until all sorts of Eiffel Tower-shaped objects in the sex-shop windows take my breath away. Whoa! I tilt my head to try to understand how that would work . . .

I wish I didn't blush when I accidentally make eye contact with Blaine at this point.

When I studied the map back in Bennett's I was pretty sure that Pages of Paris was miles away from this area. All we can do is keep walking and we end up right back in a square that looks very familiar.

'Wait, haven't we already been here?' Blaine frowns when he recognises the building with pretty shutters he'd taken a photo of earlier.

There's a round little newsstand. The kind I've seen in films. This time I can't help but take my own photos on my phone. It's so cute.

Okay, here goes. My first attempt to speak French in France.

Make Madame Fowler proud. *C'mon, Paige.*

I approach the kiosk and spot a rack of maps.

'*Bonjour! Um, c'est combien?*' That means how much.

The man inside the little pocket of magazines and crossword books and cigarettes says a number that I don't immediately recognise, so I have to sing the counting song we learnt in primary school to work out the price.

'*Ah! Oui, s'il vous plaît!*'

Delve into my pocket for money.

Feel around but can't find it.

Shove my sunglasses on top of my head so I can see better.

Mum actually hates it when people put sunglasses on their heads. She says it's a sure-fire way to tell if somebody's a tosser or not.

I reckon the kiosk man thinks I'm a tosser for taking so long.

Oh God. I am a tosser. I can't find my money anywhere.

I pat myself down. No, it's not here. Handbag. Side zip. No!

I know I put it somewhere safe.

No! The case! It must have slipped out of the case.

Fling it open. I chuck the tarantula tights out on the floor. Root through the dresses and jumpers.

'Um, Paige . . .' Blaine's looking at me like I'm possessed.

'Here, hold this.' I pass him the small pile of books I brought with me.

Some people might argue that bringing so many books on a short trip where you're guaranteed to bring back more books is unnecessary, but I get so excited about these things that I can't not have them with me.

Wish I felt that on it when it came to not losing my money.

It's gone.

I can feel my cheeks go all blotchy and hot. I don't want to cry. *Do not cry, Paige, not yet.*

'*Pardon* . . .' I try to explain with hand motions and rubbish broken GCSE French to the kiosk man. He shakes his head when I offer my bank card as payment. He's looking at me like I've put a pair of my knickers on my head and sang the Spice Girls' greatest hits at him.

To be fair, I have kind of strewn my pants all over the magazines. I can just about make out Kim Kardashian's face peeking from beneath a pile of my belongings.

I'm so gutted that I've lost Mum's money. After forking out for this *stupid case* and shopping for mini travel-sized toiletries, I know I don't have very much money left on my card. I usually try to put a chunk of Bennett's money into another account on payday, so that I have some savings for uni.

Uni. Oh, here comes that black feeling of dread. That squeeze round my ribcage like I've somehow turned into a puny sachet of ketchup.

'Blaine?' I turn to find him buried in my book, stroking his chin, all lost in thought.

The Woman Destroyed. Jeez, there's really no need to read that when I'm right here, destroyed, LIVE and in front of you!

'Pssst! Blaine!'

'Oh, hey.' Wow, he was miles away.

'Could you lend me some money? I think I've lost mine.' I grimace.

'Oh, yeah, man, I totally would, but I don't actually carry money.' He nods to nobody in particular.

Did he just call me MAN?

'Yeah, I only have my card too,' I say.

'I'm trying not to buy things. Like, I don't want to contribute to or partake in consumerism. I'm trying to live outside of capitalism.'

'So, let me get this straight –' I take a deep breath, kneeling on the floor in my absolute failure of a suitcase – 'you don't use money? Not just because you prefer card; you just – you're opting out?'

'Yeah, totally.' He runs his fingers through his hair and narrows his eyes like what he's saying is about to rock my world. 'I've just been doing it for the past month basically.'

The kiosk bloke is watching, beyond bewildered. I should just gather up my things and get up off the floor but I can't stop myself from picking.

'But, Blaine . . . can you see the hypocrisy in saying you're not contributing to capitalism . . . when you work in a shop? Selling things? And getting paid?'

'I do what I can, y'know.' He shrugs.

Is that why he stole the books from Bennett's last summer? Ugh, it still makes no sense and goes back to him being nothing but a privileged boy who picks and chooses ideals or principles when he thinks it'll make him look cool.

Actually, come to think of it. 'Can you give me my books back please?'

'*Pardon, monsieur!*' I shove my life back into my lifeless case, sling the hugging jumper back round it and ask him for directions to Pages of Paris.

LIKE I'VE died and
GONE TO HEAVEN

'OMG! Look!' It doesn't matter how cream-crackered I am after traipsing around for what feels like for ever to find this place. I don't care! Now that we're finally stood in front of Pages of Paris I feel like squealing and cartwheeling (not something I'm actually physically capable of) and jumping for joy. 'Blaine . . . we made it! We're here!'

'Cool.' He nods. His eyes are like those fizzy pick 'n' mix flying saucers as he takes it all in. I *think* – I can't really be sure – but it *looks* like he might actually be impressed. It's not an expression I've seen on him before.

Funnily enough we're much closer to the newspaper kiosk man than I'd expected, so seeing him and reliving my suitcase disaster will be a fun daily ritual I'm sure.

I look up at the famous hanging sign above the door. PAGES OF PARIS. I can't believe I'm really here. I'll be covered in bruises with the amount of pinching myself that I'm doing.

Out in front of the shop there are stalls of second-hand books. They're calling me. I'm sure that if I could close my eyes and concentrate hard enough I'd actually hear little whispers coming from inside all their dusty yellowed pages. The thing is, I can't close my eyes. I couldn't bear to close them with all of this wonder before me.

We walk over the threshold and into an actual fairy tale. I've always thought that anywhere with wooden beams is fairy-tale worthy and this place is held together with those and with ginormous towers of books that look like they're part of the architectural structure. I've never seen so many books. New and old, in different languages, on all sorts of subjects, stacked together to create this sort of Jenga dream.

Two men stand behind the counter. One is wrapping an old hardback in cellophane to protect the cover and the other is taking a long slurp of coffee from behind the book he's reading. He's wearing a yellow cardigan. I think it's probably safe to say that, no matter where you are, a bookshop isn't complete without at least one member of staff wearing a cardigan. It's an unofficial dress code.

I clear my throat and approach the desk. Okay, Paige,

here we go. 'Um . . . *Bonjour! Je m'appelle Paige. J'habite à Greysworth en Angleterre . . . et je travaille dans une librairie . . .*'

'Oh, hello! You're here! It is so great to finally meet you!' The cardigan man greets us in an American accent. He has a big beard sculpted around his twinkly smile and reading glasses hanging from a beaded grandma-style necklace. The specs rest on his knitted chest until he peeps through them to have a proper look at us. 'Please, let us help you with your luggage.'

Oh dear, my disaster of a suitcase hasn't gone unnoticed then.

'I'm Johnny,' he says, shaking my hand, 'and this is my partner, Paul.'

'For my sins!' Paul has a familiar Essex-y accent and skips over to kiss us on both cheeks. He's wearing a Virginia Woolf T-shirt. 'We're huge fans of your Bennett's Bookshop gang in Greysworth.'

'No way, really?' Blaine asks, genuinely surprised.

'That's crazy,' I add.

'Audrey! They're here!' Johnny calls across the shop excitedly.

A girl climbs down from a ladder. A proper bookshop ladder. You know the kind that Belle swings around on in

64

Beauty and the Beast? We don't have those in Bennett's, but this is definitely what bookshop dreams are made of. I've always wanted a go on these, the way I like picturing myself using a fireman's pole (even though I always slodged down the ones in the playgrounds right after failing at the monkey bars).

'You must be Paige Turner! We've heard so much about you!'

Wow. I feel like a celebrity. It's quite nice really, being this far from home and getting recognised for something other than 'Oh yes, I remember when you were only this high, and you had the curliest hair out of all the tots in playgroup!'

'Hi, thank you. It's so cool to finally be here. I've wanted to visit your shop for a really long time, so this is an absolute dream come true.'

'I'm Audrey. I'm staying here at the moment, so we will be sharing a room upstairs.' She's French and pronounces it Aud*ray*, not the way they say it at home or on *Corrie*. She's so . . . striking. She's older than me and Blaine, but younger than Johnny and Paul. She has a mane of jaw-length curly black hair and very thick dark eyebrows. Underneath all her theatrical, punky make-up, her eyes are an icy pale blue. Piercing. They remind me a bit of the big husky that lives a few doors down from mine back in Greysworth. It's called Donna. There's something wolf-like about Audrey. Something quite Donna about her. Her skin is red and blotchy, and she has a few acne scars on her chin, but she's painted a heart-shaped beauty spot on her right cheek, Marie Antoinette style. I'm immediately inspired by everything I see in her.

'*Branché!*' I read that it means cool in one of the French textbooks at school, but judging by the puzzled looks on my new colleagues' faces it's ancient grandad-worthy terminology and it's going straight in the bin.

'I'm Blaine.' He holds out his hand to shake, the zips on his leather jacket jangling.

'Ah, nice to meet you,' Audrey says, smiling. 'So were you involved in the protests to save Bennett's Bookshop too?'

OMG, how squirmingly awkward. What is he even supposed to say to that? *Well, nah, not really. I helped a lil bit with Paige's petition, but ultimately nearly screwed it up for everyone and nicked a few books while I was at it.*

'I did what I could.' He shrugs and smirks.

Ugh. Whatever. I wander off, letting their conversation fade into background noise along with the jazz playing from an old record player at the counter.

There's a wall of framed newspaper clippings about

the shop. Photos of famous writers and celebrities with their arms round Margot. She's long gone, but I feel like I know her somehow.

A socialist utopia masquerading as a bookstore . . . is what one of the headlines calls it. I run my finger over the words. It says that the shop actually opened over one hundred years ago and belonged to somebody completely different before Margot took over. She started her career as a Saturday girl and when the shop was left to her she ran it just the way she wanted it to be. I read on. *For many years the shop doubled as an informal living room for some of the most celebrated figures in contemporary literature.* It lists names. Ernest Hemingway and F. Scott Fitzgerald, Jack Kerouac and Allen Ginsberg and Anaïs Nin. The list goes on and on.

'Is this all true? Did these people really come here?' I ask, star-struck.

Audrey nods, standing beside me to look at the mounted frames. 'Oh yes.'

I can't begin to get my head round the idea that those people really existed, let alone stood right here where I am now. It means I immediately share something in common with them. How cool is that?!

'This place has been home to so many people over the

years. We have regular volunteers who write . . . Who knows, maybe they'll be famous one day.' Audrey shrugs, her eyes glazing over at the old photos. 'Come, I'll show you around.'

Audrey gives us a tour of the shelves, much like Adam did on my first shift at Bennett's, pointing out which books go where, and how they organise the sections. As Blaine and I follow her she talks.

It's even more beautiful than it looks on Instagram. Who knew that was even possible? I thought social media was supposed to be a big fat liar, plying us full of unattainable standards. It turns out it's not even doing Pages of Paris justice.

'Margot always said she wanted to create this shop in the same way that someone would create a novel,' Audrey explains as she leads us through the maze of shelves. 'Meaning that each room is like a chapter. Not all these spaces have doors, but they have these little arches you go through, see?' She demonstrates, ducking under a shelf and leading us to an entirely separate little nook of more books. It's basically a series of tunnels and books. You could completely lose yourself in a book here, instead of being distracted by Mr Abbott yelping about pig farming and the German navy, as you would be at Bennett's with our current seating arrangements.

'Margot wanted this to feel like opening a book. We step into this room, we start a new story, we enter a new world,' Audrey explains and Blaine and I both *ooh* and *ahh* in appreciation.

'That's Marcel.' She points to a man buried in a laptop, white apple glowing. He barely looks up and she tells us, 'He helps out here; he's been working on a novel for five years and won't let anybody read it.'

We come to the cafe. It's modern and light in contrast to the rest of the shop, buzzing with people who are chatting and reading and drinking and writing. There are low squishy sofas and indoor plants and mismatched vintage tables and chairs. It's very cool. They have a special menu of drinks named after literary legends. I don't really like coffee. I like the ones you can get in Costa that come with ice and lots of whipped cream and caramel syrup. They only have a little hint of coffee. Adam at Bennett's says they hardly even count. I'm not even that keen on the coffee-flavoured Revels to be honest. They can stay at the bottom of the packet with the raisins as far as I'm concerned. I'm not a big coffee drinker, not *yet*. It's something I'm going to have to get into as a chic, independent woman in Paris. I scan the list of options on the blackboard. The loopy joined-up handwriting is so nice. Is everything just more beautiful in Paris? *Oui, c'est vrai!*

'You can help yourself to any of the pastries and sandwiches that are left at the end of the day,' Audrey says and Blaine says something like *safe*. I bet he thinks it's safer than safe, seeing as he loves not paying for things.

I'm not choosing anything that comes with milk or syrup today. Nope. I'll have an espresso. Go hard or go home. I ask the woman in the Pages of Paris apron for a Molière.

Audrey taps her chin with her finger, furrowing her wolfy brows in concentration. 'What else do I need to show you . . . ?' She's wearing chipped green nail varnish.

'I love your outfit.' I marvel at her and gather myself before dissolving into a puddle of total fandom.

'Oh.' She looks down at herself, like *this old thing*, as if she hasn't just stomped off the end of a catwalk for London Fashion Week in a black-leather skirt and fluffy mohair jumper that is the exact colour of Pink Panther Wafers.

'Oh, yes, look at this. It is the schedule of events we are running in the shop.' Audrey points to an enormous hand-drawn blackboard calendar. It's amazing. There are workshops and readings and even a life-drawing class (GET IN!!!!). There's a feminist book club and listings for some kind of avant-garde experimental musician who is doing a residency.

'Margot opened her shop and her home to many different book-loving travellers on one condition; you must work for two hours a day and make sure that you read every day. We keep this up in her honour. You do two hours here and the rest of the time is yours. Because it's voluntary, many of the people fit it around other jobs or studying, but we all spend a lot of time in the shop, because there are so many cool things to join in with. Who would want to be anywhere else?!'

'You're so lucky to be part of this,' I gush.

'Well, you can count yourself lucky now – you're part of this too.'

'I suppose we are . . .' I beam. 'It's just there's nothing anyway near as cool as this at home in Greysworth. Apart from Bennett's, it's a bit of a hole.'

'A what?'

'A hole?' I say, embarrassed that I can feel Blaine laughing behind me.

'What do you mean?' Audrey asks, smiling. 'I'm sorry. I don't know that word.'

'It's just a bit rubbish basically. The town.'

'Ah . . . yes. People can be very small-minded in small towns.' She tells me she left home when she was my age and has travelled all over. Now she's living and working in Pages of Paris and trying to write a play. 'I have no intention of leaving any time soon.' She laughs and sticks her tongue out at Johnny.

'I used to come here all the time when I first moved to the city. Margot was so cool. I mean, she was very eccentric. She lived alone, here above the shop, and she never had any children. She'd tell me the books I was reading were no good and push her favourite novels into my hands. She was unwell for a number of years before she died. A few of us who knew her through the bookshop actually visited her the last time she was in hospital. When she passed away it became clear that she hadn't made plans for what would happen to the shop . . . I couldn't bear to think that it would close for ever.'

'So what did you do? How did you form the co-operative?' I ask, weaving through the bookcases and towers of books that pile up on the floorboards with my paper cup of very strong, very hot espresso.

'We all met here outside the shop the day Margot died. We put our minds together, worked out who would like to help and who had a few hours to spare here and there. We came up with a plan and moved in.'

We reappear from behind another book tunnel and head back to the cash desk.

'The demand for this shop has always been here, so we didn't struggle to sell books after she passed,' Johnny chips in. 'And I think that because this place is here out of pure love and dedication they'd rather come to us than buy books online.'

'Yes,' I say, nodding. That's what every Bookshop Girl likes to hear.

'So all the money that we make goes back into the upkeep of this place. We have to make sure we have enough to put on workshops and pay performers. You'll meet a load of volunteers over the next few days; it's a revolving door.'

'And everyone's lovely!' Paul says, 'Well, *mostly* every-one . . . !'

'Oi!' Johnny nudges him and barely suppresses a giggle.

I think I'm going to love it here. They seem like a nice bunch, which is important. I've been lucky enough to work with Holly and Adam, which is always a laugh. Obvs we talk about books a lot, but we can also spend days on end debating whether Jaffa Cakes are biscuits or cakes. (Despite arguing about this at length on the shop floor, I don't honestly know where I stand with Jaffas. Sure, they say 'cake' on the packet, but it's not like you need a plate or a little fork or a napkin to eat them. And the sheer volume at which they're consumed is way more biscuit-y than cake-y.) Thankfully this feels like a shop full of Holly and Adams rather than a shop full of Tonys.

'Sit with us! Have a biscuit,' says Paul, patting a space on the reading sofa next to him. He and Johnny tell us about how they met each other and fell in love at Pages of Paris, and swap stories of Margot from back in the day.

'Oh God, once she caught me reading sad love poetry in that chair . . .' Johnny points and laughs. 'I was so heartbroken that I asked her if she had ever felt heartbreak. Can you imagine that?! How obnoxious! Asking somebody that!'

'No you didn't!' Audrey howls.

'She said yes, she knew heartbreak. I asked her if a heart could heal, and if she had found love since. Go ahead, you can laugh – my twenties were as tragic as they sound! That's when she told me: *you never go to bed alone with a book.*'

'She was cheeky.' Paul smiles, his eyes wet with laughter. 'And she was wise. Everything she told you was a quote from something she had read. As she got older her references got more muddled up, but you could see it ticking over in her head . . . She could recite poetry and Shakespeare soliloquies; she was still doing that in her hospital gown, wasn't she, John?'

'And she was integral to so many literary scenes over the

years. She was a real icon. And she'd encourage everyone to write while we were staying here.' He points to the old typewriter tucked away at a desk amid the shelves. 'That thing hasn't worked for years!'

'We could never get rid of it.' Johnny sighs. 'It's an important part of this place, even if it's seen better days.'

'Haven't we all!' Paul says with an eyebrow so perfectly arched it makes me think he must draw them on or have them microbladed in a fancy salon.

I cannot wait to tell Holly all about this. I also cannot wait to pee any longer. I've needed the loo for at least the last hour and a half I wasted getting here with Blaine. And now I'm bursting, thanks to the coffee and the excitement of actually being here.

'Excuse me, could you tell me where the toilets are?'

'Oh, of course!' Audrey chimes. 'Then I'll show you to the bedrooms upstairs.'

I can't believe I'll be sleeping in the bookshop. It's the kind of thing dreams are made of. It's the kind of thing *books* are made of!

I lock the bathroom door and dance over to the loo. The walls are baby blue and decorated with hand-painted clouds that all have little cherub faces. This is the cutest wee I've ever had. I suppose it's also the most momentous wee I've ever had. I tend to think that every year, to be fair. On the eve of my birthday I'll think *This is the last wee you'll ever do as a fifteen-year-old*, then, the following morning, my mind will be blown by the thought that *This is the first wee you'll have as a sixteen-year-old*. This is my first Parisian pee. This is the first time I've used a famous toilet. I wonder who came up with ideas for their ground-breaking novels perched here on this bog? Maybe some of that genius will rub off on me and I'll come up with the best personal statement known to UCAS. Especially if I get to go to a life-drawing class IN PARIS. That'll really give those snooty admissions people something to read about, dahhhhling! I wonder if Blaine will bother going to that; he hasn't been at Posers in Bennett's for ages. I pull at the loo roll, worrying that I've spent too long lingering and that my new colleagues will think I'm a weirdo and I'd die if Blaine thought I was in here for anything other than a wee.

ROOMIES

'Here is your bed.' Audrey points to the single mattress by the window. It has orange paisley sheets and one of those knitted granny-square blankets folded over the top. There are floor-to-ceiling bookshelves and creaky wooden floorboards. It's an Instagrammer's dream and one of those *life-changing magic of tidying*-er's nightmare. I think the clutter is beautiful.

'I sleep here.' She bounces onto her bed. 'Oh, and this is Simone.' A fluffy white cat slinks onto her lap and she strokes it lovingly, blowing her cigarette smoke away from its whiskers. 'She is old, and too slow to catch the mice, but she is a good listener.'

'The mice?'

'*Oui*, there are mice everywhere in here. They've been here longer than you and me, but they are harmless.'

Oh God. I can pretend I don't think it's rude that she's smoking in the bedroom. I can even pretend to like cats, but can I actually pretend that I think mice are harmless?! Can I fool myself into forgetting that they carry all those germs and disease?

'Wow, this place is amazing . . .' Blaine appears at the door to our room, gazing around at the bookcases like a kid at Legoland.

'You stay in the attic room?' Audrey asks him as the cat jumps from her lap and mooches round Blaine's gangly legs.

'Yeah, I'll be upstairs. It's great.' He beams. 'Nice one, Paige Turner.'

It makes me want to vom seeing him all pleased with himself. It should have been Holly stood in that doorway, petting Simone and running her fingers over the dusty spines on the shelves.

'I'm going to a bar tonight. To see my ex-lover's band play. Do you want to come along?' Audrey asks me, all eyelashes and cheekbones.

'Sure.' Blaine cuts in.

Well, it's not like I can say NO just because he's going. This trip is *my destiny* after all, right?

'*Génial!*' Audrey smiles and it's electric. 'I leave you to unpack, then I'll meet you in the shop downstairs.'

*

The book treasures in this place are UNREAL. Oh! The treasure! It doesn't really matter that my suitcase wheeled into this place in tatters; with all the new books I've coveted so far I'll need a brand-new Louis Vuitton-esque trunk to carry it all back home with me.

So far I'm being very well restrained. I mean, I'll need to be, seeing as I don't have any money. I've only bought an Arthur Rimbaud postcard for Holly. I'll make sure I get round to writing that ASAP. How I'll fit everything I want to tell her onto a postcard I do not know. There's a spinner display of cards and a whole load of them are portraits of famous authors. I count the ones I recognise and test myself (only in my head, not out loud – don't worry, I'm not a total freak) to see if I can name something written by them. I make a note in my sketchbook of any writers I haven't heard of so I can track their books down and see if they're for me or not.

A few customers mill about in the aisles. A couple hold hands as they browse the stalls outside, using their free hands to pick out books for each other. Their palms are cemented together. They make it look effortless, though. Like a beautiful, romantic version of the three-legged race at sports day, without the shouting or the plimsoles.

I sigh. A Parisian sigh.

Being part of a co-operative is the best, especially when everybody is as cool as Audrey, Johnny and Paul. It feels so NICE not having a grumpy manager like Tony telling you what to do. I kind of wish somebody would tell Blaine to *do* something other than leaning on the counter, though. It's a bit frustrating. Whatever he does is frustrating.

VINTaGE FRIPERIE

I need to make every moment that I'm in this city count. I'm going to try to hit up a gallery every day that I'm here. Johnny said he and Marcel the laptop guy would cover the shop so that we could have a lunch break with Audrey before going back to Pages of Paris this afternoon to learn how to use the tills. Sure, I've been reprimanded for being late back from lunch in Greysworth and really there is no excuse for that . . . it's only usually because I've got deep into enjoying a Toffee Crisp and have lost all track of time or have spent an eternity in the Superdrug queue while they offer ever single customer a spritz of the same cut-price Katy Perry perfume. This will be different.

I've studied the map of the Metro, and, despite the fact that it looks like a massive tangle of Christmas tree lights, I think I've worked out that I can get to most of the sights and back within this little window of time. I've got to make sure I have plenty to bang on about in my personal statement. That'll shut Mr Parker up. Wipe the know-it-all look off his face.

Ooooh, wow . . . a shopfront catches my eye. It's so pretty. They have the most beautiful nineteen-fifties satin dress in the window. The waist on it is tiny, like it belongs on top of a cake, like it's made from icing and buttercream. I can't resist. I'm one step away from pressing my nose against the glass and steaming up the windows. *Maybe we could take a teeny-weeny detour, just for a second . . .* I think, then feel Audrey pulling me towards it. Blaine follows along behind us.

Friperie is the French word for a second-hand shop. We have one vintage shop in Greysworth called Nan's Boutique. It opened a couple of years ago and has some all right stuff, but it's mostly Eighties jumpers with massive shoulder pads, and I've even found a couple of things with Primark labels, so I usually have more luck finding treasures in charity shops. Mum says she can't believe stuff from the Eighties counts as vintage. I can't believe anyone would choose to wear blazers and call it fashion.

This shop does not look like the charity shops at

home. Inside it's rammed with rails and piles and stacks of denim and polyester and cowboy boots and handbags and fur coats. I run my fingers over the mink stoles until I remember that they once belonged to real life animals with beady little eyes and sharp teeth, and it makes me snap my hand away in horror. There's an old vintage dressing table with a mirror and it's decorated with shiny brooches and chunky clip-on earrings, lace gloves and pillbox hats. The walls are plastered with retro magazine clippings and sixties dress patterns. I wish I could take everything with me.

I still feel rubbish for losing my euros this morning, so anything I buy here will be eating into my pitiful uni account . . . and I've tried so hard to set a bit of Bennett's cash aside for that but, oh God, I want to buy something from this magic emporium. Mainly, mostly just because I cannot wait for somebody at home to compliment me on my new garm' so I can say, 'Oh, this? Thanks, it's vintage. I bought it in a little boutique in Paris . . .'

I'M SO READY FOR THE GLAMOUR.

Blaine is taking pictures of the shop. Really, he has nothing else to do since he's not contributing to capitalism blah blah blah, yadda yadda . . . I hope they have CCTV cameras in here because you never know what he might shoplift. Maybe he'll mooch out of here wearing a flouncy feather boa and 1920s smoking jacket. He's a seasoned pro when it comes to five-finger discounts after all.

Audrey holds a big netty wedding dress up by the hanger. She looks like she's considering it. I wonder if she's getting married or if she'd just wear that to work a shift at the bookshop. Her style is pretty 'out there' from what I can see so far. I think she looks great. Nope. No bridal gear today, she decides, as she dumps somebody's best-day-of-their-life dress back on the rail and screeches it away from her.

There's a tall wooden hat stand with fuzzy berets in every shade displayed on it. Wow . . . Well, *when in Rome*!

I squint at myself in the mirror as I pull a beret around on top of my head, trying to see if I can make it work.

I hope the previous owner of this beret didn't have nits. It's kind of itchy but I think that's just the woolly fabric it's made of.

'Hmmmm . . .'

I scrunch my face up. Unsure.

'*Quoi?*' Audrey slides a pair of oval nineties-style lime green shades down her nose to look at me.

'Oh. Just. I don't know if I can pull this off . . .' I'm still squashing my hair under the hat, wondering whether the fringe should stay in or out of it, when Blaine leans over a huge pile of old acid-wash Levi's.

'You can pull anything off, Paige Turner.' He flashes a smile and I swear that smile is more dangerous than wearing belly button piercings on the death-trap trampolines in PE.

There's a sign by the big old-fashioned till saying they take cards. That seals that deal. Shut up and take my money, *monsieur*! *S'il vous plaît!*

Blaine asks me where I'm going after this, his leaning arms folded on a bulging rail of psychedelic nylon shirts with massive pointy collars. Why are his eyelashes so long? It's obscene.

'I'm going to the Louvre,' I say like it's no big deal. I expect him to tell me that it's overrated and that he's been there a bunch of times, but Audrey beats him to it.

'You two have fun. I'm taking these –' she waves the green sunglasses at the shop assistant – 'and I'm going to meet my friend for a coffee. I'll see you later. Good luck getting around the Louvre in an hour!'

God, I bet we seem like such dumb tourists to her. A couple of lamos. Basics on tour.

Hang on, when did me and Blaine Henderson become 'you two'? Ew.

Is he just going to tag along with me everywhere I go?

Jeez, I feel like Mary and her little lamb. Except my lamb is all tall and boyish and does photography as a hobby. Which I imagine would probably be pretty tricky if you had hooves.

CULTURE VULTURES

I let Blaine take a picture of me in my new fuzzy beret stood by the front of the Louvre. I feel a bit weird and self-conscious posing for him. As a rule I don't like other people taking photos of me. It's not like I'll throw a diva-like strop every time my mum wants to take a pic of me blowing my birthday candles out or anything. I just still feel like I did on school photo day in front of a camera – awkward. And Holly's notes on the back of her school pic is proof that Year Four really is the cut-off point for looking cute in those things. Selfies, on the other hand, are a totally different kettle of fish. I take a few of my own selfies to send to Holly and Mum. *Beret l'amour* as the caption. Pretty sure that doesn't even make sense, but it sounds nice.

I gaze at the shiny glass pyramid of the Louvre.

I can't believe I'm actually here. It's cool to be in front of something you've only seen in books or on telly. From out here it does look like the set for the kind of old game shows they replay on that Quest Channel. I feel like I know the pages of the DK guide to Paris off by heart. Like the description of the collections in this place are the lyrics to my favourite songs. I read that at one point Napoleon renamed the museum after himself and hung the *Mona Lisa* in his bedroom. Can you imagine that?

Maybe one day I'll call this the Paige Turner Gallery and I'll rearrange my room to fit something expensive and fancy above my knicker drawer.

After we've queued and I've had my bag checked by security and we've passed more security guards with actual GUNS, we're in. At last. It's huge and busy and overwhelming. The whole place seems to be swarming with people taking it in turns to stand in front of the *Mona Lisa* and recreate the Beyoncé/Jay-Z selfie thing.

We watch from the other side of the room. 'She's actually pretty small. I kind of expected it to be . . . y'know, bigger and fancier.'

'Ah, Paris syndrome . . .' Blaine points a finger at me and smirks.

Nope! There's no way I could be disappointed by this

place. It's amazing. I don't think I've ever been anywhere so full of people who want to be in one place. It's tourist central. There are groups of people following tour guides waving mini flags in the air. There are others listening to big old-fashioned headphones. There are people wearing backpacks on their fronts, cradling them like big waterproof babies. Some people are holding cameras way above their heads to take photos of the famous paintings in an attempt to crop out the sea of baseball caps and scalps.

'It's too busy to see anything properly here . . .'

I'm thinking out loud, panicking that we need to make the most of this in the short time we have before we're due on the tills at Pages of Paris. I don't want to let anyone down, but I also *need* to tick this off my list. I want to get at least one observational drawing down in my sketchbook. Proof that this really happened. My arm will go blue if I pinch myself any more than I already am. I can't just show them *that* on my personal statement. *Believe me, I was really there. Look! I have this beret and all these is-this-really-happening pinch marks to prove it! Please consider my application blah blah blah. UGH!*

'Let's go this way.' Blaine leads us through another big hallway. I bet he's been here *a bunch of times* too. I let him take charge this time and this time only.

We march through the gallery, shoes tip-tapping on the shiny marble floors. I lose count of all the cherubs and rosy bum-cheeks and golden swirly hairstyles we pass.

Ah. Now this, *this* is beautiful. Serene. A room filled with huge white sculptures. Bright and airy, much quieter than all that hustle and bustle.

Blaine crouches next to a marble statue of a woman. She's nude and lying down in what looks like a really uncomfortable position. I take a closer look. She's resting on a bed of flowers, all really intricately sculpted, and there's a tiny slithery snake wrapped round her wrist. She's writhing in pain after being bitten.

Wow, can you imagine how embarrassing it would be if you were stuck, forever immortalised, squirming in agony with your bum out, in a museum where people get right up close to you to have a look? Imagine if *this* was your claim to fame. Obvs I know she's not real. This whole composition would have been staged in a studio somewhere a long time ago. They'd have used models and made preliminary sketches and practice runs. I think Mr Parker said they're called maquettes. The little mini versions sculptors make before they go on to executing the real deal. I lean closely to read the label. I bet *Auguste Clésinger* intended for this to be sexy. Maybe it is. I mean, she is beautiful. Even if she's in pain she looks like a total babe. Her face is peaceful and her hair is perfect. I reckon being chomped by a poisonous snake in real life would make you pull some pretty unflattering expressions. Like when you accidentally open your selfie camera and are suddenly staring into your own ugly thumb head with a set of multiple chins. It's a bit silly for a man to think that this is how a woman suffering in pain should be portrayed, but it was made all those years ago, and the way it is made . . . is exquisite. I love coming to galleries and looking at art because it makes me think words like *exquisite* to myself, and it makes me laugh because nothing in Greysworth could ever be exquisite.

'What's funny?' Blaine says, smiling. I was miles away, LOLing out loud about my telly art critic monologue I had going on in my head.

'I'm just really happy to be here,' I say, sighing.

Another Parisian sigh. I'm getting into them.

Back in my head: even though they're cold and the scale of these stone figures is way bigger than any actual living person, I still feel like they could come to life any minute. Like if I glare at this chick with the snake for too long she might just turn her head and say 'Oi, you could at least HELP me if you're just going to stand and stare!'

While Blaine takes black-and-white film photos of the delicate rolls on her twisted back, I perch on one of the velvet benches and get my sketchbook and pens out.

My right hand gets to work without me even thinking about it. I draw quickly to get the legs and the stomach down. It's not like she's actually going to wobble like Big Sue does in Posers life-drawing classes back home, but I stick to my usual technique – get the shapes recorded onto the paper first, details coming in after that.

Blaine sits by my side and starts doing the same thing. When I glance over at his work it looks like he's spending a lot of time drawing her boobs. *Groooan*. Can marble breasts really be that interesting?! They're made of stone! There's some heavy graphite shading going on, which is pretty unnecessary in a room as bright as this.

On my sketch I draw a speech bubble coming out of her lips. *Stop looking at my tits.*

Before long our silent draw becomes a side-by-side chat. We talk about drawing people from real life and drawing stone.

'There's no blood beneath the skin. Everything is smooth and cold. It's almost like it's dead. Frozen in time.' At least I'm not the only one who gets all overexcited with arty-farty chat when I'm unleashed in a gallery . . .

'Yeah.' Agreed. 'It's kind of a bit like drawing furniture,' I offer.

He frowns, like he's considering what I just said very carefully. Wow, okay. It's not like I'm playing this down or anything. I can see that this sculpture is a masterpiece that undoubtedly required a huge amount of skill and time. I'm hardly comparing it to a shelving unit from IKEA or anything. I let him babble on about *freezing time* and yet I feel like I can't say anything to him without it being taken way too literally.

Silence.

'Why did you stop coming to Posers?' I don't take my eyes off my marble subject.

I've been thinking about this for a while. After the occupation to save Bennett's, the day that I realised Blaine had been shoplifting from our shop the whole time and that he was not the friend-slash-potensh lover I'd hoped he'd be, I didn't see him for months. Holly said she'd spotted him doing some community-service litter picking in the town centre, but he hadn't been back to life-drawing classes and nobody knew where he'd disappeared to. Not even Beige Clive or Big Sue.

As much as I consider him to be a total idiot, maybe he might have felt really uncomfortable hanging around me after that day at Bennett's. After all, I did tell him to get lost. It was a proper public dressing-down, one I'm admittedly still proud of, but sitting here now I'm wondering if it made him feel small. Ashamed of himself and his actions. Maybe I made it hard for him to come back, which wasn't what I'd set out to do.

'Posers?' He shrugs. 'No reason, other than I was over it. I'm good at drawing people. I know how to do it, so I didn't need the practice any more.'

Wow. For a second I'm sure I just saw the statue of snakebite girl move. Like she propped herself up on her elbows after hundreds of years just to say 'Oh God, Blaine Henderson. Get over yourself!'

Well, I guess there are no deeper levels to his character. I suppose he doesn't feel bad about what happened at all. It's not that he couldn't face the crowd at Posers; he just thinks he's the mutt's nuts when it comes to observational drawing.

'Then why are you here now?' I ask without even knowing I wanted to know that.

He laughs, hand on his chest pretending to be offended. 'Why am I *here*? Why are *you* here, Paige Turner?'

I feel my face flush at him using my name.

'Okay. I want to see this.' I wave my brush pen towards

94

the sculpture. 'I want to see all of this. All of the art and the museums and galleries and places I feel I've missed out of my whole life living in Greysworth. I need to prove that I can be here in these places and that I'm good enough to get into uni . . . I've started feeling kind of worried about it . . .'

WHY am I doing this? HOW am I opening up to Blaine and WHY can't I stop it from happening?

'Really? Why?' He blinks at me.

I physically can't stop. It's like someone without a driver's licence has hijacked my mouth and taken it for a joyride around the Homebase car park.

'Well, the teachers make it seem like your personal statement is the most important thing in the world, and like it's going to be really hard for us to get anywhere and I just— What's so funny?'

He shakes his head, laughing.

'You shouldn't listen to a word teachers say. They're full of crap. And they're only there to control you.'

I let that wash over me. It's not like I'm a total teacher's pet or anything, but I doubt even the really annoying teachers are trying to control me.

'And as for the personal statement, that's a farce. Nobody will even read it. It's really unimportant. You shouldn't let it get to you.'

'Sure. Okay. Thanks, Blaine. Wow, you're amazing; you've cured me of all anxiety,' I say sarcastically, 'I mean, maybe for you it was unimportant because maybe you were guaranteed a place at uni. Some of us have to *try* at things. Maybe, well, I guess you probably *knew* someone who got you a place, right? Like you *know* somebody who can just get you a job at Bennett's.'

I feel embarrassed for even saying that. I feel hot and tingly all over, like I'm the one who's been bitten by a snake. He looks away from me. Back to his sketchbook. I shouldn't lose my temper at him. It just makes it look like I care. Which I don't by the way. I couldn't care less about him. He's not worth getting worked up about.

'Well, just *say how you really feel, Paige. Don't hold back,*' Blaine mutters.

Maybe I should gather my materials and make up an excuse to leave.

Silence. Awkward silence. Just the sound of pencils on paper. One of the dinner ladies at primary school used to say that silence meant an angel was passing by. I mean . . . if angels spend their time watching an assembly hall of snotty kids eating Cheestrings and Müller Corners I think I'd rather go to hell.

A tour group enter the hall from the other side of the

room and I'm actually grateful that they're here. Something to break the awkward silence at least.

He's laughing again. Is he insane? Are my feelings really that hilarious?

'What is it now?'

'I was actually trying to be nice to you.' He shakes his head. 'You don't have to worry about that stuff. You're good. At drawing, I mean. I've seen your stuff.'

I can barely mutter a thank-you, and it's not because I'm bad at taking compliments; I'm just bad at saying sorry.

He pulls the top leaf out of my sketchbook. My snake speech-bubble lady.

'Take this for example.' He holds it up in the air, looking at it like he's Beige Clive in the crit at the end of Posers. Now he's tacking it UP ON THE WALL OF THE GALLERY with a piece of masking tape from his little pencil tin of materials.

'Blaine! What are you doing?!' I hiss, hoping nobody will notice what he's doing.

He ignores me completely and continues, waving his arms around dramatically and putting on stupid voices. 'When admissions at UAL, the Royal Academy, Brighton, Cambridge . . . wherever it is you want to go . . . when they see your name they'll say "*My word, it's Paige Turner. World-famous Paige Turner. Exhibited in the Louvre alongside masterpieces by Da Vinci! Monet! Vermeer!"* Their work pales in comparison to yours . . .'

'Shut up!' I blush and laugh. And hate myself for laughing.

While it's funny to see him taking something less seriously, this is turning into some horrible game of piggy in the middle (which is always a horrible game come to think of it). He holds his arms out at a distance, so that I can't reach my own drawing from the wall.

'OMG, what are you doing?! You can't do that!'

Before I know it I'm barged out of the way by a group of tourists who are all looking at my sketch! NO!

Blaine stands back, beside himself with laughter. HELP! Oh God, what has he done? This is so embarrassing.

'Excuse me! Uh . . . *excusez-moi?*' I try to get closer to the sketch to grab it back, but it's as if a mosh pit of people dressed in linen and sun hats has formed between me and 'the piece'.

Do they really think this is part of the exhibition?! How could they possibly think that a drawing *I* did, with pens I bought in WH Smith (after haggling the price down because the packet was damaged and one of the fine liners had been nicked) – a drawing that features a speech bubble which says 'Stop looking at my tits' – how could they think that was intended to be seen on this wall?!

This cannot be happening. They're taking photos on their SLRs. Some are uploading it onto their Instagram stories. I'm stunned. And for a moment I totally let go and fall about laughing at how mental this is with Blaine.

ON THE RUN

I'm actually crying. Cry-laughing. My cheeks hurt, my face aches. Wait until Holly hears about this; she won't believe it.

An even bigger crowd has gathered to look at my stupid sketch. It's getting more attention than the sculptures. This is crazy.

Oh. Uh-oh.

I dab the tears of laughter from my eyes, careful not to smudge my eyeliner. Oh no, I think we might be in trouble. A gallery attendant with a walkie-talkie is marching towards us to see what the commotion is all about.

'Blaine . . .' I whisper. 'What are we going to do?!'

The guard looks at the wall, looks at us, and, without saying a word we both run.

Ohmygodohmygodohmygod. This is bad. I hate running.

I've never even tried *out*running anyone before.

He calls after us, and we turn a corner, into a huge mass of people in one of the main rooms.

Wow. This is stunning. Huge floor-to-ceiling masterpieces in heavy gold frames that make you feel like a Borrower line the walls. There are throngs of people craning their necks, the way you have to in the front row of the cinema, to take in the paintings.

'Slow down,' Blaine whispers. 'Just try to blend in.'

For a moment we bob along with the other tourists, and I'm still keeping an eye out for the guard until we come to a famous oil painting I recognise from the guidebooks.

Liberty Leading the People by Eugène Delacroix. Whoa. This is one of the most dramatic pictures I've ever seen. It stops me in my tracks and I'm transfixed by Liberty herself: the huge powerful woman leading the people in the French Revolution. She's almost golden, moving through the smoke and the gunpowder, holding a gun in one hand and waving a French flag in the other. Her bare feet step over the corpses of dying soldiers, as she leads scruffy Artful Dodger lads with guns and fancy men in top hats to freedom. It's wild. Obviously in real life there was no muscular babe fannying about with a big flag while the people took to the streets to fight for revolution; and if it was true and she was, then I imagine she'd have avoided wearing a strapless dress prone to falling all the way down past her belly button. It's just not practical. Liberty has her boobs out in the painting. Naturally. Of course she does. *Stop looking at my tits.*

I'm lost thinking about how cool it is to be here in front of such a famous painting that so many people have stood and looked at over the centuries, when all of a sudden I feel somebody tap me on the shoulder.

'This way, Paige.'

Blaine takes my hand and we scarper. Weaving our way through the crowds. I can just about see his face in front of me and he's laughing. This is all fun and games to him. Maybe we should just own up. I don't actually want to get into trouble. I don't want a revolution. I'm no Lady Liberty; I don't have a big flag and I'd rather not expose myself to any of these guided-tour selfie sticks.

We pass another gallery attendant who glares at us as she listens to the message crackling through her walkie-talkie. I smile nervously. *Be cool, Paige.*

When we came in here the security guards by the entrance of the museum were pretty serious. They weren't the kind of slouchy, yawning high-vis blokes we have roaming the Grosvenor Centre in Greysworth. Oh no.

They were even more on it than the guards they have wheeling around on those Segway things in Milton Keynes. They all looked like real life Action Men. They had *guns*. I hope they don't actually gun us down. That would be embarrassing. At least I'd be too dead to cringe. Or can you cringe from beyond the grave? Oh God, what a waste of my last precious breaths on this earth!

Gulp. We have to get out of here. I walk as fast as I can, but all my guidebook knowledge of this place has packed up and ditched me. I have no idea how far we are from an exit and I don't think stopping to ask a member of staff is a good idea right now.

We manage to creep off again before ducking into a dark room. It's pitch black. Silent and still. I can just make out the silhouettes of a few people sat on the benches watching a slide show of artworks projected onto the wall ahead. It takes a while for my eyes to adjust to the light and I'm struggling to get my breath back, like I'm the last person to finish cross-country.

I feel really aware of how hard I'm panting, so I try to hold it in but that just makes it worse. My heart is beating so hard that I'm almost certain everybody in this room can hear it. And the fact that Blaine Henderson is stood so closely to me in the dark. Smelling that way he does.

Of leather and chewing gum and cigarettes. He held my hand earlier. Sure, it was during a getaway attempt, but *he held my hand*. This isn't helping my breathing at all.

How are we going to get out of here?

Breathe, Paige. I try to concentrate on the screen ahead. I don't know what we've walked into, but it seems to be a presentation about the depiction of HELL in Renaissance painting. I suppose I'd better get used to all this fire and torture, because I'm going straight to hell for today.

Oh God. The man with the lanyards and walkie-talkie, the one who spotted us in the first place, is hovering by the entrance and looking right at us.

I try to avoid all eye contact, to focus on the projection like it's the most exciting thing I've ever seen.

I nudge Blaine, who is watching the slides, arms folded like maybe he is actually really fascinated by it.

What are we going to do? This place is a sanctuary, but if that guard is waiting for us, then at some point we'll have to leave this room and where will we go then?

Crap. He's coming this way, sneaking in but making a beeline towards us.

Oh God, I don't know what he's saying; he's whispering in French. I just freeze. I'm stunned into silence. Now is obviously an ideal time to not even pretend that I can't speak French. I don't think I can speak any languages at this minute in time. He's obviously trying to avoid disturbing the peace for the other people in the room.

His walkie-talkie beeps and crackles, and some other voices echo out of it and one of the women watching the film on the bench tuts, turns round and grumbles at us, and the guard waves his hands to apologise to her.

We stand in silence for a moment. I have no idea what to do. I open my mouth. Then close it again. Then Blaine grabs my arm and runs. I don't even feel my legs move but we dart across the small dark room, the projector catching us and flashing Renaissance depictions of HELL across our heads.

At this very moment a demon is projected onto Blaine's face, its pointed tongue curling at Blaine's cheekbones and I am certain that this can only prove this boy IS the devil himself.

Crowds, tour groups, selfie sticks, they all blur into one as the thick rubber soles of my Doc Martens slap across the marble floors.

It feels as if all eyes are on us. I can totally imagine all the marble sculptures coming to life and pointing at us. Dobbing us in to security. *There they are!*

We run out of the museum so quickly that I don't even

have time for my heart to break over missing the gift shop. Everyone knows that's the best bit of any gallery. All I wanted from the Louvre was a sketchbook fresh with observational drawings and a few postcards. All I've left with is a stitch and a brush with the authorities.

We don't stop running for what feels like miles. My throat is burning and my heels feel red raw inside my shoes, but I'm scared to stand still in case they catch us.

'Paige. Paige! I think we can stop now.'

Blaine is doubled over. Hands on his knees. Hair flopping into his eyes.

I turn to him, gasping for air. His head is upside down. What the hell just happened?!

I tell Blaine we should just try to act casual when we roll into the bookshop. It's an actual Bible-worthy miracle that we made it back here on time. How I can manage to be late back to Bennett's after a forgettable tea break wandering the desolate Grosvenor Shopping Centre, while in this city I can fill my sketchbook with observational drawings, fit in a spot of vintage shopping and be chased out of the world's most famous museum neatly within the hour, I'll never know. Maybe that's just the magic of Parisian time.

'So how did the sightseeing go?' one of the bookshop

volunteers asks. She's an older lady with dyed orange hair and glasses on a cord round her neck.

'Sure. Oh yes, great. *Génial!*'

WHaT'S FRENCH FOR 'THE DRUMMeR IS FIT'?

Whoa-Em-Gee. Wait until Holly hears about this. A gig, in a basement bar in Le Marais, wall to wall with Parisian fitties. So this is it, *this* is where they must all hang out, in the dark damp caves beneath the streets. I imagine the David Attenborough impression I'd do for Holly if she was here now. One of our favourite things to do when we're observing somebody without them knowing it is to make it into an imaginary nature documentary and do the commentary.

Welcome to Fit Planet. *Tonight we'll be examining the habits of an increasingly endangered species – the fanciable drummer . . .*

Audrey said she liked my dress, which is my favourite thing to happen so far today – and, oh boy, has it been an eventful day. Paris makes me feel like I'm living inside a snow globe that someone's given a good shake. I'm wearing my sixties sparkly silver-lurex minidress with some red patent boots I got in the sale at Topshop. My cool Parisian roomie introduced me to some of her friends, including a boy called Max who said '*Bonsoir*' and kissed me on both cheeks. I know that's just a thing that people do here, but the thrill of physical contact with somebody so gorgeous (even if it is pretty nan-level on the scale of sexy intentions) was quite something. It's obvious that everyone loves Audrey. She has queues of admirers. Just this afternoon at the shop a sulky-looking boy asked me if she was working today. I told him she'd gone to buy cigarettes. He looked like Audrey could have gobbled him up and spat out his bones. He also looked like he'd kind of love for her to do that. Now she has her arms round a tall boy wearing all black everything. He's very beautiful. I wonder if that's her ex-lover?

Note to self: when I'm older I'm going to refer to boyfriends as lovers. It'll make me seem worldly.

Everybody's drinking beer in little glass bottles. I decide I'll try one too. It's disgusting but this is very exciting and that outweighs the taste.

Okay . . . so there's a bit of thumb twiddling to do on my part while I wait for the band to start. The room around me is very lively but . . . it's just hit me that I've somehow ended up on a night out with Blaine Henderson, and I think he's ditched.

I suppose this is a bit awkward being here with nobody to talk to. I've never gone to a gig by myself before. So actually this is a first. It's the kind of thing only a tuff chick independent woman would do. Maybe I could sling this into my personal statement . . . *Please consider my application. I'm really good at pretending to text someone on my phone when I'm in a crowd and don't want to look like a loner . . .*

I've got my book in my bag. Sod it. I'll read. When in doubt – read.

Somebody is leaning over and talking at me.

'How can you see what that says in the dark?' Blaine. Bottle of urine-flavour beer in hand. 'Unless you have X-ray vision or something.'

'Don't you mean night vision?'

'Yeah. That's what I said. Isn't that what I said?'

'You said X-ray vision. That would be seeing through stuff, not reading in the dark.'

'Fine.'

A pause.

Then we both start saying different things at the same time.

'You go,' I offer.

'Nah. You go.'

'What d'you think is better, X-ray vision or night vision?'

'There's some stuff I wouldn't want to see in the dark.' He wrinkles his nose and takes a swig of bin juice beer.

'There's some stuff I wouldn't want to see through either . . .' I shudder on purpose.

'Like what?' He laughs into his bottle.

'Like . . .' I only have to think for a second. 'There's this regular Bennett's customer called Mr Facer who wears one of those really smelly wax jackets. He always has a load of Morrisons bags for life with him, and when he pays he has all his money in an assortment of dirty envelopes and packets. Once he fished a load of five-p coins out of an old Branston pickle jar. It was so gross.'

'Oh my God, that's grim.'

'I don't ever want to see through the Morrisons carriers. I do not want to even think about the contents of those bags. So you can take your X-ray vision, I'm not convinced.'

I know we're covering a pretty niche subject here, but I also know that I'm funny. Blaine's attention is elsewhere, however. I turn to follow his eyeline. He's watching a girl on the other side of the room. She's wearing a long flouncy dress and her hair's all shiny.

Boys are disgusting.

The buzz of the amp plugging in makes my knees wobble. Three skinny tall boys with shaggy hair slink onto the stage. There's one girl in the band; she plays keyboard and doesn't smile, not once. Too cool.

They start playing and the whole room vibrates.

I pay close attention to the crowd. Everybody stays still. There's some very subtle swaying and a little nod here and there, but mostly everybody just pouts and sips whatever drink they're holding. It's not like the gigs we go to back at home. Every now and then a decent band will play in the back room of The Racehorse in Greysworth. Everybody dances and pushes and sweats.

Fringes are ruined. Eyeliner melts off. It's a very different vibe.

But this is exactly what I'd expect from a sophisticated metropolitan crowd.

Once they finish their set, the room disperses into little groups again. Blaine is talking to flouncy shiny girl.

I don't really feel like pretending to read again. You know how people say you can feel like a little fish in a big pond? Well, I totally get that, standing here aimlessly. Except I don't feel like a little fish. I feel even smaller than that. Like the weird in-between-y tadpole with front legs that comes somewhere in the middle of those Life Cycle of a Frog diagrams. Wet and newty, and a bit odd.

What would David Attenborough have to say about me now? I think it's time for me to head back to my natural habitat: books.

My phone pings. It's a photo from Holly. A postcard! Writing so tiny I have to zoom in on the pic to read it.

Well, you haven't even been away for twenty-four hours and I am already SO BORED without you! Can you BELIEVE that I went to Oxfam today and found an old Walls ice-cream tub filled with THESE BEAUTIES! Postcards of Greysworth in its heyday (if Greysworth has ever had a heyday . . .). I've never SEEN a postcard from Greysworth before, so naturally I bought them ALL! Expect a familiar eyesore for every handwritten exchange. First up is a photo of our beloved market square in the seventies. I hope you're having the most beautiful, glamorous, bohemian adventures in the city of LURVE! I cannot wait to hear all about it – so please don't make me wait! Tell me EVERYTHING! Hol xxxxxxxxx

MOUSE!

Back at Pages of Paris and I have my room to myself.
I wonder if Audrey will stay out with her ex-lover tonight.
They looked pretty loved up to me. I've got the room to
myself. I know exactly what I'll do.

I jump to my feet and start exploring the bookcases
round the room. There are so many books packed into
this space. Stacks on stacks. Spines squeezed in sideways.

There are books in all kinds of languages too. Maybe I
should try to read something in French, just to show off
to myself.

I slide a book out of the shelf and that's when I see it.

It darts from behind the bookcase and runs behind a
tower of books piled up in the corner.

A MOUSE.

Ahhhh! It was massive. It wasn't like those cute Disney

ones from *Cinderella*. It wasn't wearing a little T-shirt and cap. It was big and shiny and MEAN.

Oh God, what if it's a RAT?

I jump up onto the bed and hug my knees to my chest. I do NOT want to see it again, but I also cannot blink because I don't want to miss it.

It moved so fast.

It's like I can't stand to look at it, but at the same time I want to see exactly where it is.

Scratching. It's making this horrible horror film scratching. Does it do that with its teeth? Or is that the sound of its nasty little claws?

I hear the floorboards squeak, footsteps up the stairs, past our bedroom door and further up. It's him. It's Blaine. He's back.

I know I'd rather stick this rodent torture out than ask HIM for help. I'd rather be eaten alive by the mice than ask him for help. I'd rather they made my rotting corpse their forever home and used my empty eye sockets as mini mousey Jacuzzis than ever ask that boy for help.

I curl up on the mattress, pull the sheets over me so that it's impossible for them to provide any kind of ramp for mice to climb up into bed with me. I put my earphones in and scrunch my eyes shut.

NOOOOO!

I JUST FELT SOMETHING LAND ON TOP OF ME.

A LARGE MOVING, LIVING, BREATHING CREATURE.

OH GOD.

I freeze under the weight of this thing. It has to be the biggest demon rat to ever live. I'll end up as one of those weird clickbait articles that pop up on social media. GIRL SUFFOCATED BY GINORMOUS PARISIAN MUTANT RAT.

Whatever it is it's making this strange kind of purring sound . . .

Oh.

I yank the covers away from my sweaty face.

'Simone!'

Phew! That cat. Thank GOD it's just the cat.

'Seriously, you scared the life out of me! What is it? Do you want me to stroke you?' She curls up on top of the covers. 'Okay . . . well, only if you promise to catch all the mice in the shop for me. You don't have to kill them, if it's against your beliefs or whatever. But I'd really, hugely appreciate it if you could have a word with them. Get 'em gone, Simone.'

Simone is a strange name for a cat. Such a human name.

I had a friend in primary school who called her pet hamsters Barry and Keith. Weird. It's just like having two furry little old men run about in a cage full of sawdust in the corner of your room.

Could this mangey old cat really be the true reincarnation of Simone de Beauvoir? Do I even *believe* in reincarnation? I guess there's no way of ever knowing, right? If it's true, then what would I like to come back as? A bookshop cat is a pretty good deal, I suppose. I hope Blaine comes back as a toilet brush or a foot file.

She purrs. It's cute.

Maybe it's some kind of sign. 'Although if you are the real Simone de Beauvoir, then you wouldn't really believe in *signs*, would you? You're all about me shaping my own life by my own free will . . .'

I feel a bit like Dr Doolittle as I stroke her little cat forehead tentatively.

'Well, Simone, if shaping the future of this trip with my own free will is all up to me, then I've really been screwing it up so far . . .' I stare into her huge green eyes, waiting for answers. 'What am I supposed to tell Holly? I can't exactly send her a postcard telling her I'm spending my first night in Paris holed up speaking to some weird cat – sorry, no offence – who may or may not be the reincarnation of one of literature's finest existentialists, after a long hard day being chased out of one of the world's most famous art galleries . . . can I? Maybe Holly would have been here if I hadn't fiddled with the names in the hat . . .'

Me and Simone yawn at the same time.

'Stay here . . . you'll protect me from the mutant rat, won't you . . . ?' Even if she's too slow to actually catch any of them, hopefully they can smell her cattiness through their little mousey noses and will stay well back.

I can feel myself drifting off to sleep and murmuring to Simone. I guess I'm not totally alone in this city if I have her.

COVER GIRL

I wake up. In Paris!

I'm in Paris! In the seconds before I remember I'm scared to death of my rodent roomies and that I'm semi-mortified about yesterday's events in general, waking up in my Bohemian Fantasy is beautiful.

I sit up in bed, kicking my feet out of my funky vintage sheets. Simone has buggered off. And there's no sign of Audrey. Oh God, maybe she had to get away from my snoring. Mum said I snore like an old man. I said that saying that just reinforces gender stereotypes. She said I hadn't let her finish and what she actually meant to say was that I sound like an old man with a peg leg moving furniture around on a wooden floor.

I hope my nostrils haven't betrayed me. I'm TRYING to be cool. Audrey is without a doubt the coolest person

I've ever come into contact with.

I run to the bathroom with my towel and lock the door before anyone can see me in my bed-headed morning glory.

I look at my reflection in the mirror and have a word. 'Paige. This is a brand-new day. You're in Paris.' I laugh at that but, yes, it's true. 'No drama today, okay?'

Maybe not everybody speaks to their reflection. My mum always does this thing she saw on a film when she's applying lipstick; she'll say 'Oooh, you've got lovely lips' to herself. This obviously runs in the family, and who am I to fight genetics?

Is it weird to stop halfway through shampooing my hair to think that I'm standing right where Blaine must have stood this morning? I stare at my wet feet on the retro blue tiles and wonder how his gangly tall body was somehow squashed into this cubicle? If he's up, I mean; he could still be asleep.

Yes, Paige, it's weird.

I pick a nice outfit out of my sham suitcase, tie my hair into a big bun on top of my head with a bow and do the 'lovely lips' thing in the mirror as I put on a pinky-tinted balm thing.

It's a new day. The sun is shining through the huge old windows and the book dust is dancing in the rays, and, as far as I can tell, not a creature is stirring, not even a mouse.

I practically skip down the spiral staircase to the shop. I feel like Belle in *Beauty and the Beast* when she's skipping through the streets, with the baker and all his mates popping out of their houses to say '*Bonjour!*' I cannot wait to clamber up that bookshelf ladder and channel all my animated cartoon Disneyness today.

Audrey is setting up the shop, getting ready to open up. It's incredible; she's gone for a completely new look today. Her dark hair is tied up on top of her head in a big red velvet bow. It's like she reinvents herself on a daily basis. She's the Lady Gaga of bookselling. She introduces me to a boy in dungarees who's wiping down the counter and frothing a cup of oat milk in the big shiny coffee machine. *Je m'appelle Paige* . . . His name is Luc. It's so cool to meet all the different volunteers. It's just cool being around other book people.

I ask Audrey if there's anything I can do to help, and she shows me how to set up the stalls outside the shop. I'm unpacking box after box of second-hand treasure onto the trestle tables. At this rate it feels like I'm counting *one for Pages of Paris, one for me* with every paperback I unload.

There's no comparison is there really? Paris and Greysworth. Paris is a place where people want to *be*.

A place people travel from all over the world (and even endure Eurostar journeys sat next to obnoxious boys with fancy cameras) to get here.

The sun is shining down on me in my bookshop heaven, making the buildings in the square look like they're made of shortbread biscuit and those wrought-iron balconies are shiny liquorice. It's a crispy, bright day. This is the life. I take a deep breath and smell something so delicious it deserves a cartoon smell hand beckoning me over.

Crêpes! Mmmm! I spot the little cafe across the square. *Oui, s'il vous plaît!* I know I'm in a world of delicious pastries that are culturally deemed more appropriate for breakfast, but it just struck me: I can have whatever I want for breakfast, lunch or dinner. I could have breakfast food at teatime. I could have a Viennetta for brekkie if I felt like it; nobody's going to stop me. I'm an independent woman in Paris. I guess this is what it'll be like if-slash-when I go to uni. I can't wait to banquet on whatever I want when I want. I'll order pizza for breakfast. I'll have Ice Cream Factory with all the toppings and sauces for tea. What could be more exciting than culinary freedom?

I watch the lady in the cafe make a crêpe in one hypnotic, swishy motion. I have it with Nutella and banana and whipped cream. I shovel the hot spongey heaven in my gob quickly. *Let them eat crêpes*. It's so delicious and fresh that I think I can safely say eating this crêpe is the happiest three minutes of my life so far. I'm savouring the last mouthful as I take a look at the French fashion mags at the little news kiosk in the square.

There's a boy on the cover of one of the magazines that looks a bit like Blaine. Dark quiffy hair, swollen pouty lips, moody. He's leaning against a wooden stool with a leather jacket flung over his shoulder and the words JEUNE HOMME MODE printed in big bold letters across his body. It's weird to think that Blaine is the only other person to know about yesterday's gallery fiasco. I mean, even though he is my sworn enemy and happens to be The Most Obnoxious Fittie Ever, we shared *something* and if one of us dies or goes senile like the old lady in that crappy Ryan Gosling film *The Notebook*, then the other person will feel like it was all a dream and have to question whether it really even happened at all or not. Whatever. That was yesterday, this is the here and now. I'm just a girl in Paris, with a bellyful of crêpe, and a bookshop to play in . . . right after I've had a proper look at all these shiny bougie mags . . .

The kiosk guy in the hatch is really staring at me. I mean, yes, I know that maybe having the audacity to come back here after the suitcase-tights debacle is pretty brazen, but there's no need to eyeball me so hard . . .

He's saying something to me, and I thought we'd already established that my French doesn't take me much further than ordering a can of Orangina *à la piscine*.

I try to explain that I'm just looking. Leave a person to browse if they're happy doing so; it's rule number one. I'd know. I smile politely and put the magazine with the Blaine lookalike down.

Now he's pointing. Wow . . . well, this is just rude. What is it? Have I left the house without drawing both eyebrows on again? Is it a massive bogey? Do I have snot on my face? I look around; oh God, now he's calling people over. Have I unintentionally been flicking through some dodgy publications? I thought it was just fashion and art!

A crowd of local vendors gather to get in on the action. That's when he holds up a newspaper WITH A PICTURE OF ME AT THE LOUVRE ON THE COVER.

BLAINE
'BIG MOUTH' HENDERSON

Back on my trying-to-become-a-coffee-drinker bull crap,
I order a Flaubert from Carlos, the cafe volunteer.

'How are you enjoying your time here in Paris?' he
asks as he bangs around on the big metal coffee machine.

I haven't spent enough time around coffee makers to
understand what all the percussion and shiny bits that
come out and go back in again are about. I'm sure I could
find a book about it if further reading is required.

'Oh, Paris is great! I'm loving it,' I smile, and that is
true. I deliberately leave out the bit about the struggle
I'm having to convince random newsagents that I'm not
the girl pictured on the cover of a national newspaper.
Once the flat-capped bloke in the kiosk had finished
waving that blurry CCTV image of me in my beret at the
Louvre in my face, I basically just ran back over to Pages

of Paris to hide and pretend this isn't really happening.

'Oh, wow. That makes a lot of noise!' I shout over the hiss and splutter of the coffee machine.

'This thing?' He laughs, eyes creasing into little crescent moons behind his hip tortoiseshell glasses. 'It's ancient. On its last legs for sure.'

The same could be said for lots of things at Pages of Paris, but maybe that's what makes it so special. I hope it sticks around for ever, but it feels like part of the magic lies in the dusty shelves and the creaky floorboards.

'So . . . it may be old and noisy, but it still makes a good strong espresso.' Carlos pushes a small red cup and saucer of Parisian SOMETHING my way.

'*Merci beaucoup!*' I hold it to my lips and blow to cool it down.

It smells like Maths teachers.

I wiggle over to the newspaper rack to take my first sip. Just as I think *Here's to you, Mr Langston. Thanks for trying, but I still have no idea what Pythagoras was on about*, I spot another newspaper with yet another snap of my gallery-busting face all over it!

The espresso spurts out of me before I can do anything about it. I'm like a horrible shopping-centre fountain spraying out coffee. It tastes like soil. How do people enjoy this?

But HOW DO I STOP THE CIRCULATION OF EVERY FRENCH NEWSPAPER is the real issue.

I slam the cup onto the counter in an attempt to grab the tabloids with my museum CCTV face on them and hide them, BIN them, unaware that (of course) I'm being watched.

'Is it really that bad?' Carlos winces.

'No! No. It's just. This paper is old. It's dated from yesterday. Old news! Can't have that, can we? No. It's all right. I'll get rid of it.'

I stagger over to the bin and shove it in. Then I immediately realise I put it in the general waste not the recycling bin so I fish it out and shove it back in the right one. I'm acting so shady. I hope Carlos hasn't noticed. I really don't want him to find out what a freak I am. Or that I'm guilty of defacing the Louvre with my sketch of a woman saying 'Stop looking at my tits'.

To think, there I was, turning my nose up at the manky old hats in the Bennett's lost property cupboard when we couldn't find a beret; when what I could really do with now is some woolly disguise to pull right down over my MOST WANTED face.

But, oh God, I cannot be arrested. That is not what this trip was for.

And I really don't think I'm cut out for a life of crime. Back in Year Seven, Mrs Jones arranged for an inmate from the nearby prison to give a talk in assembly. His name was Sky and he was beautiful. He was responsible for the sexual awakening of every single one of us sitting cross-legged in rows on the dusty parquet floor as the gruesome PowerPoint slide show of prison injuries and cell-made weapons flashed behind his heavenly shaved head. It was really something. The blood. The shanks. Plastic toothbrushes with razor blades melted into them. Toes that had been injected so many times the veins had turned black and scars from boiled water and sugar attacks. Somehow regulation jogging bottoms had never looked so good.

Sky said he'd got in with the wrong crowd. I wanted the names and numbers of these people. I wanted to get in with the wrong crowd if it meant getting in with Sky. We could go on the run. 'Bunny' and Clyde style. I thought that if we got caught, we could be bunk buddies. I'd stroke his bumpy, prickly head and he'd draw stick and poke prison tattoos all over my body.

It seemed like Mrs Jones's assembly had massively backfired. We were not at all frightened of prison or drugs or boys. For weeks I wasn't at all interested in boys *unless* they had a shaved eyebrow and an electronic tag round their ankle. But I've watched enough prison documentaries since then to realise that I wouldn't last a minute banged up. My only real brush with the law was the time I nicked a Puppy In My Pocket from Clinton Cards. My mum didn't notice until we got home. I was just sat in my pushchair clutching a small plastic dachshund. I'd like to say that's as far as it's ever gone, but *now*, thanks to Blaine Henderson, I'm front-page news and Paris's most wanted.

This is terrible.

'*Merci*, Carlos!' I dab the sticky Flaubert dribbles from around my mouth with a recycled Pages of Paris napkin. I should get on really. Keep my head down. Sell some books or something, that's what I'm here for after all.

There he is. Blaine. Leaning against the World History bookcase (and I stop to wonder if I've ever seen him stand upright), he's talking to a small bald guy with a handheld recording device.

As I get nearer I hear the guy say, 'If you could, in your own words, tell *Le Monde* what you saw happen at the Louvre yesterday . . .'

Blaine opens his mouth wide like he's about to spill ALL the Heinz baked beans to this . . . yes, I believe he is, an ACTUAL REPORTER!!!??

'EMERGENCY!' Hands fly to my mouth but it's too late, the reporter and Blaine are both looking at me before I've even decided what it is I'm going to blurt out next.

'*Excusez-moi?*' The guy with the microphone recorder-y thing blinks at me.

'Bookselling Emergency Meeting now, please, Blaine. Sorry to interrupt.'

(Well aware that I've become one of those people that says 'sorry to interrupt'. I hate that phrase and I hate the people that use it. They're never sorry; if they didn't want to interrupt, then they wouldn't. Anyway, that's not important right now. Where was I? Is it coffee that makes me feel this intense? Like I'm a walking, talking pinball machine and all the lights on me are flashing and all the flippy bits are flipping?)

I pull Blaine behind the Philosophy bookshelves by the collar of his leather jacket. 'What are you doing?!'

Still holding onto him, it suddenly feels very strange to be touching him. I let go and clear my throat while he looks at me. 'It's not a big deal. It's pretty funny actually. If you see the funny side.' He barely supresses a smirk.

'*Funny?!*' I blink. 'Funny is . . . This isn't *funny*; this is a disaster!'

'Can I just say –'

'No, Blaine, just shut up; you've said enough. I swear I've never met anyone with such a big mouth before.'

'YES. It was me! It was MY stupid drawing upon that wall! It's all right for you to laugh, isn't it? YOU'RE the one who got us into this mess in the first place and yet it's not your mug that's splattered across every French tabloid! And what are you looking at?'

I haven't got with many boys in my short time on this earth, but my limited experience in Boys Looking At My Mouth and everything I've been led to believe based on Holly's home-made TED talks proves that usually when this happens they're about to go in for a snog. Oh God. Well, not only is he sorely mistaken in thinking I'd want to go anywhere near his slippery slimy gob, but his timing is wildly inappropriate.

'I was just going to tell you that you've got Nutella . . . or something . . . on your chin.'

FReNCH RUBBER OF DESTINY

I turn to walk away from him, wiping chocolate off my face frantically. UGH! I sulk for a moment behind the counter. I rifle through the pen pot, to at least try to look like I have some kind of purpose here other than humiliating myself.

I can usually find sanctuary in stationery. Biros, a wooden ruler. A really lovely fountain pen that I write my name with a few times. An eraser. It's different to the Rubber of Destiny at Bennett's. This is sort of pinky-brown. The colour of old plasters floating on the surface of a swimming pool. With a Biro I write *OUI* on one side and *NON* on the other. C'mon, French Rubber of Destiny, I could do with a friend.

Is this entire trip going to be a disaster? Flip. *NON*.

Great. *Génial*. Not the answer I was expecting.

Am I going to get into trouble when my mum finds out I've made the French headlines? Flip. *OUI*.

Stupid French Rubber of Destiny.

Is Blaine Henderson an idiot? Flip. *NON*.

Well, this is faulty. I shove it to the bottom of the pen pot where it belongs and stab it with a Biro.

I don't even know why I'm wasting my time on this stupid rubber. What is destiny anyway? According to Simone de Beauvoir (the cat), we all have the ability and the free will to write our own destiny. It's not down to fate, or rubbers. It's down to us. Blaine Henderson is an idiot and that is entirely down to him.

Audrey jumps up on the desk behind the till and begins working through a pile of books, labelling them with a big clunky price gun.

'So, you and Blaine.' She says it just like that. You and Blaine. I freeze, dropping the stabby Biro into the pot of stationery.

What's she going to say? She looks at me steadily. She's pretty terrifying. My eyes dart around the shop, looking to see if he's nearby. He must be slumped in one of the book nooks, reading or looking at himself in a portable mirror, because there's no sign of him.

'Uh? Who?'

I don't know why I ask that.

'Your friend, Blaine. You know, the one you campaigned

with at Bennett's?' She laughs because obviously I'm acting like a weirdo.

'Oh, no way. We're not friends. I mean, we don't really know each other that well at all.' That sounds defensive. Way too defensive. 'And besides, I don't really think he deserves to be here on this trip anyway.'

'Oh . . . wow. That sounds . . . *dramatique*.'

It is a bit. I don't know what to say.

'I just wish someone else from Bennett's could have been here instead. We don't actually get on that well with each other . . . but everyone else in the Greysworth bookshop is a total babe.'

'I had no idea that you didn't like each other. You know, I actually thought maybe he liked you . . .'

'No way!' I shudder. Is she kidding?

I don't feel like Blaine goes out of his way to be mean to me. It's not like he's tugging my pigtails and calling me names, which we all know is a *totally* unacceptable way to let someone know you fancy them, and it's not like he's flinging roses and teddy bears at me either. I really do not know where Audrey got that idea from. I'm fairly certain that Blaine only has eyes for himself. Good luck to him.

'So, is there anything you'd like me to do?' I ask Audrey

to change the subject. Even though she's not a manager, she's senior to me, and she walks about the place like she knows exactly what's what with everything. She also *lives* here so . . .

'No. You don't have to ask me for permission to do anything,' she explains, 'because we all share the work here. You can read if you like. Just . . . pace yourself, have a seat and if anybody wants to talk to you about books, then make sure you talk to them about books.'

'Really? You mean I don't have to stand in a certain place at a certain time? And nobody will frown at me if I just . . . read?' I can't help but sound like someone's just told me Santa really does exist and he's asked them to chuck the keys to his North Pole toy workshop my way.

'No way! Why would you ever get into trouble for reading in a bookshop?! Is this how you work in Greysworth?' She laugh-frowns.

'Well, it's happened before, yeah . . .' I mutter. Sure, I was reading long steamy extracts from one of Minnie Rockwell's paranormal romance novels to Holly at the time, but Tony *did* tell me to stop.

'No, no, no! Paige, you are part of this bookshop. You work here now. It is as much your bookshop as it is mine, or Carlos's or . . . even Blaine's. We are a co-op. We share.

I don't tell you what to do with your bookshop just as I don't tell you what to do with your hair.'

My hands fly up to smooth my fringe. Just in case I *should* actually be told that it's gone loco.

'This is based on trust. It's collectivism.'

When she says 'collectivism' it comes out like *collectiveesmuh* and my heart does a little flip like a hot buttery crêpe ready to be slathered in Nutella.

Can somewhere so far from home and so different to what I've grown to love actually feel like home?

TELLING AUDREY

'I think it's pretty cool.' Audrey sips her coffee as she nods at the computer screen behind the desk.

'Oh? What are you reading?' I ask, looking up from my dusty hardback collection of *Female Pioneers of the Surrealist Movement*.

'You know, the thing that went down at the Louvre yesterday.'

I gulp. I feel like I must look the way people look when someone says 'You look like you've seen a ghost,' and I let out a weird little hissy 'Oh yessssss.'

'It's so funny!' She laughs. So carefree. 'In a stuffy old gallery filled with paintings and sculptures by men, I love to think that all the beautiful marble women have something to say about it.'

My God, *how* has this become something people

are talking about?! How am I supposed to keep it on the down-low and get away with it, if I have to endure conversations about it and pretend that I, *who me*, had nothing to do with it?! She watches me as I laugh nervously. I didn't mean for it to be, but it's definitely the fakest, most distracted-by-something-that's-really-bothering-me laugh to ever emanate from my body.

'Paige, are you okay?'

'Audrey . . . I. Can I, um, tell you somethi—'

A smiley customer approaches the till and asks if we could stamp the inside of the book they just bought.

'Sure.' Audrey dabs the ancient rubber thing on a pad of black ink, looking at me as if she's still trying to work out a sudoku puzzle tattooed on my forehead.

'Thank you so much!' An American accent. 'This is such a special shop. My daughter will love this!'

'*De rien!*' Audrey smiles as she waves the billionth happy customer goodbye.

I reckon now's the time to give Pages of Paris a good old tidy. Yes, I'll just throw myself into work to avoid any more awkward yes-it-was-me-I-did-it-please-don't-tell-my-mum conversations. I collect a load of books that have been waiting to be shelved behind the counter and pile them into my arms. I may as well throw in a whistle to make this all seem as casual as poss.

'Paige.' Oh, great, she's following me down the Books About Paris aisle. 'Where are you going? What did you want to tell me?'

She rests her hand on my shoulder and it makes me stop.

'It's me!' I whisper through gritted teeth. God, I hope she doesn't throw me out of the shop for this. Tony will murder me if he finds out I got flung out of a bookshop that doesn't even have a manager on flinging duty.

'What's you?' She sniffs me. Like I've farted or something.

'No! Not that.' I waft her away.

'Then what are you on about?'

'I mean.' I check that no customers are lurking or listening in. 'It was me. At the Louvre. I'm *la fille au chapeau.*'

'Ah, *oui*.' She nods.

Huh?! '*Oui?*'

'I know you're her. Duh . . .'

I feel my eyes pop out of my head. 'What? You knew it was me all along?'

'Yes. Obviously. I see the photograph; I know it's you. Straight away, no doubt.'

'Oh.'

'The girl in the hat. Paige, I was with you when you bought the hat in the *friperie*.' She laughs.

I feel my insides melt like butter on toast. 'But you didn't tell anyone!'

'Why would I?!' she sings. 'We're roomies. We're here to protect each other.'

'Phew! Well, I'm glad you feel that way, because I'm gonna be sticking around here for the rest of the week. Inside, where it's safe. I cannot go back out there,' I say, shaking my head and pointing towards The Outside World. 'I don't like all the attention. I don't like people saying what I drew is "disgraceful" . . .'

'You can't hide here for ever, Paige. It didn't work for Quasimodo and it won't work for you . . .'

GUERILLA GIRLS

Oh God, what's she doing? Dragging me out into the daylight. Doesn't she know I'll melt or vaporise or whatever it is that vampires do? She's giggling like this is some kind of cute kooky scene from *Amélie*. No thanks. I have to draw the line on silver-screen stereotypes somewhere.

'There's a book here I want you to see.' She's flipping through big art books on the trolley by the front of the shop. '*Excusez-moi*.' She gets to ask customers to move out of her way. That's wicked. We're not supposed to do that at Bennett's. Tony says it's bad customer service, but I've literally stood behind a browser for a solid fifteen minutes, waiting for him to decide on a diabetes cookbook, just so I can reach for a calorie counter someone's reserved over the phone. It's torture.

Just nudge them out of the way. Polite, but forceful. It's so simple! This will be one of the things I'll enlighten my Greysworth colleagues with when I return, brimming with knowledge and wise anecdotes from my time 'on the continent'.

'You've heard of the Guerilla Girls before, right?'

'No . . .'

'Ah!' Audrey is excited when she gets to show me something new, and instead of feeling stupid for not knowing, like I sometimes do back home, I can't wait for her to show me. I'm opening up my head ready for her to pour Cool Stuff into it and swill it around like the slush machines in the corner shop. 'I think we have something here . . .' She taps her fingertips along the spines on the shelves of the Art bookcase.

'Basically they're a group of female artists who formed in the Eighties when they were fed up of the sexism they were experiencing in the art world. Yes! Here it is.'

I flick through pages and pages of funny colourful posters, billboards and . . . gorilla masks. 'What's with the masks?' I wonder out loud.

'That's how people knew it was a Guerilla Girls appearance or performance. That's their thing.'

They look a bit scary, but it also looks kind of fun.

They're making a point loud and clear, but they're having a laugh while they do it.

I hold the page open on a picture of a flyer, which Audrey tells me is one of their most famous pieces. Bright yellow and pink. It shows a nude woman's body reclining as they often do in classical art, with a big gnarly gorilla head on her shoulders. In big bold lettering it asks 'Do women have to be naked to get into the Met. Museum?' Then: 'Less than 5% of the artists in the Modern Art Sections are women, but 85% of the nudes are female.'

Wow. It makes me think about how I felt drawing the snakebite sculpture. *Stop looking at my tits*.

'So, who are the women inside the masks? Are they famous artists?'

'Well, nobody knows. It's top secret. They hide their identities and do things as a group because they believe the cause is more important than anybody's individual identity. They're disguised in their monkey masks . . . a bit like you are in your beret, *la fille au chapeau* . . .' She pokes me in the arm. Luckily she didn't go for my BCG otherwise I'd have turned into an actual gorilla.

I close the book and give it The Stroke. The stroke everyone does in that moment that you decide you want this book; it's yours. You hold it in your hands and you stroke it. Hello, new treasure. You're mine. Obviously The Stroke is universal and they do it here in France too, because at this very moment Audrey says, 'Go on, I want you to have this.'

She did this on purpose, didn't she? Audrey flicked the switch on all the light bulbs in my head. I must be glowing up there, running up a massive electricity bill, like the house on Spinney Hill Road that goes waaaaay OTT on the Christmas decorations at the start of November. We'll actually take a detour on the way home from school just to stand and watch the big inflatable Father Christmas dangle from the guttering.

'Thank you, Audrey. *Merci beaucoup*. For the book and the food for thought.' My tummy growls. 'Speaking of food . . . have you had your lunch break yet? Where can I buy some stinky cheese around here?'

OMG, Paige, this sounds amazing! I love the Rimbaud postcard. Do you think he was fit? Is that a weird thing to say? Today's Greysworth special is a gorgeous photo of our beloved bus station before it was demolished. Glorious! Not a patch on the things YOU must be seeing. So the French exchange booksellers are both pretty nice BTW. I feel kind of sorry for them swapping the city of love for the city of . . . lard. Today I took Sabine for her first Greggs. I think that once she got over the initial trauma she actually enjoyed her sausage roll.

Holly xxx

TUMBLeWEEdS

Honestly. It's true. I Google-translated 'posers' from English to French and it turns out it really is just *Les Posers*.

A lady called Mademoiselle Gigi has arrived to lead the class. Everybody knows her; they're all bending at the knees to kiss her on both cheeks and shake her small wrinkly hands.

Audrey leans on my shoulder to whisper in my ear. 'You're in for a treat, Paige. These classes are legendary. Mademoiselle Gigi is somewhat of an institution at Pages of Paris . . .'

I watch her move through the shop. She's got orange hair. Bright orange. The kind you'd get teased about by idiot boys for having at school but then absolutely LOVE when you're free from folding rulers and protractors and PE kits and could probably become a model for one of those hairdressing competitions they always seem to be having on BBC Three programmes. It's a huge mass; it must be Rapunzel length when she lets it down, but it's piled up on top of her head, like a big cloud made from Wotsit dust. She looks like she's probably quite small underneath all the huge scarves and pashminas that wind across her shoulders, and she walks with a stick, pointing it as she talks.

'*Bonsoir.*' Mademoiselle Gigi smiles at me and says something like '*Je ne crois pas que nous avons rencontré . . .*'

I flick through the tattered pages of my hand-me-down-school-textbook French. I think she's saying we haven't met before. So I try my best. 'Oh, um, *bonjour . . . Je m'appelle Paige. J'habite en Angleterre.*'

'Ahhh! An English girl! I know England; in fact, I lived in London for some time during the sixties.' She winks at me. The eyeliner around her big amber eyes is so thick and heavy that I think it must be tattooed on.

'Are you here for my life-drawing class?' she asks, pulling a large roll of paper out of one of those old lady shopping trolleys.

I nod, relieved that my limited French skills won't stop us from talking. 'I'm looking forward to this class. A lot. I'm actually staying here in the bookshop this week, upstairs in one of the dorm rooms.'

'Ah, I see, you're a Tumbleweed!'

'A Tumbleweed? *Qu'est-ce que c'est?*'

'Oh, yes! You see, that's what Margot used to call the travellers who lodged here. They were usually at a very particular stage in life . . . looking to find their path.' Her eyes narrow at me mischievously. 'And, oh, she loved meeting booklovers from all over the world and offered shelter to anyone who needed it. She'd only ask that while you stayed, you'd write up a one-page autobiography on the old typewriter.'

I know the one she means. It's a relic with a handwritten sign Sellotaped to the dusty old keys that says NE PAS TOUCHER S'IL-VOUS-PLAÎT/PLEASE DO NOT TOUCH.

'I think there must be an awful, embarrassing passage written by my former self buried among the rubble here.' She chuckles, her lungs rattling.

'So you knew Margot? And you were a Tumbleweed too?'

'Well, I wasn't officially a Tumbleweed. I never slept here, although I slept all over back then.' She laughs again and it turns into a hacking smoker's cough. 'I spent a lot of time in here nonetheless, and Margot became a good friend of mine. As women who lived and loved for books, we were kindred spirits.'

'That's very special,' I whisper, in awe as Mademoiselle Gigi continues to haul pots of inks and brushes and one of those tacky lacy Spanish fans and a big box of wine out of her somehow glam granny trolley.

She takes a deep breath and smiles. 'Bookshops are magical places. I love them. When I was a young girl I got a job in a bookshop and I fell madly in love with a boy I worked with. It was a very long time ago . . .' Her round eyes widen and she giggles. 'But every time I come into a shop like this and I smell the books, I can feel myself falling in love again. I feel like a girl again . . . How do you say . . . ? I'm weak at the knees!'

'Oh . . .' I melt. '*J'adore.*'

I know it makes no sense and I probably look like a right loser but it's all I can think to say and it feels completely natural.

'Well, if you love bookshops, then you'll love Paige,' Audrey sings. 'Paige has led her own "high-street revolution" back in Greysworth. She's a real rebel girl . . . We are very excited to have her here.'

'A woman after my own heart,' Gigi croaks.

I think this is the bit where I'm supposed to say something like Oh, *please, Audrey, stop! You're making me blush!* But the truth is I don't ever want this to stop. I feel like the whole room is spinning. This is the best night of my life and these are my people. RIP me. I've really died and gone to heaven. Gigi just referred to me as a WOMAN. So long kidulthood; sophisticated lady world, here I am.

Audrey asks me if I'd pour some of this *vin rouge* into a row of plastic cups. Sure, why not? *Pourquoi pas?*

It's a huge carton with a little plastic tap attached to it, so decanting it is actually quite fun.

So far I've never really been able to say I like red wine. I've only had a sip of it when my mum's offered it to me, and wasn't mad on it, but I'm pretty sure that it will become a staple of my life at art school so I'm going to have to practise. I'm determined to learn how to be good at liking it. Along with coffee. I'm sure I'll still guzzle my way through litres of Vimto if I ever get out of Greysworth, but I'll make sure I leave room for sophisticated beverage-inis too.

We scrape odd chairs across the shop floorboards, arranging them for the life-drawing visitors in a bit of a hotchpotch. It's like it is at Christmas dinner, when you have to borrow extra seats for all the extra people and end up plonked round the table at different heights because somebody's perched on an emergency footstool.

Once Pages is buzzing with sketchbooks and easels and people wearing big flouncy scarves, I squeeze into a good spot next to the Women's Studies shelves (deliberately, obviously). Oh – here we go, the bit when the life model starts to derobe. This is always a strange moment. No matter how much practise I've now had with drawing people once they're in the buff, the process of them undressing hasn't got any less awkward. You can't help but feel like looking at this stage would be weird or leery or pervy, but having a good observe once they've let it all hang out is perfectly acceptable. I catch him wriggling out of his baggy harem pants. They're huge parachutey things, with a sort of batik, tie-dye elephant print on them, that defo look better scrunched up in a heap on the floor. The hum of the class dies down as we start to pay attention and think about how we'll translate what we see in front of us onto the paper in our sketchbooks. *Translate* is a word I've picked up from Posers back home. It's the kind of thing I'll shove into my personal statement to sound serious and arty.

'Just like old times.' Blaine slides a chair up beside me.

'It's not at all like old times,' I grumble.

'What?' He leans over, all tall, dark and infuriating.

'I said, no, it's not like old times at all –'

'*SHHH!*' A man sitting behind me, who is clearly taking this class VERY seriously, makes his point. My cheeks go all hot because it feels exactly like getting told off at school and I'm immediately guilty for talking and passing notes all at once.

Well, that's it. Enough. I'm not letting Blaine get me in trouble again.

I get my head down and begin to form the overall shape of Victor, our Poser.

Old times. It's not like old times. Not one bit. For a start this bookshop is the most beautiful place I've ever been. It's hard to concentrate on just drawing the naked man because really this whole room is worthy of having its portrait done. And, secondly, my favourite Greysworth life model, Big Sue, would never keep a pair of flipflops on for the entirety of her pose like this bloke. It just looks plain weird, like he might wander out of the shop at any minute and roam the streets of Paris with his big hairy bum out. Maybe he'd sit and get a caricature done by one of the artists outside the Sacré-Coeur. Or plonk himself down on one of those plastic chairs outside the crêperie with zero lap protection from hot, oozing Nutella as he watches the world go by . . . Maybe I should sip this red wine a bit slower. It's taking me to places I'd rather avoid.

Life drawing back at home, at Posers, has made me more comfortable with looking at bodies and seeing shapes and shadows rather than WHOA-THERE GENITALS and BUMS. Drawing people as they sit right in front of me is now something I find relaxing, especially here, in Paris, sipping wine with a Pages of Paris institution in the room. My bohemian fantasies are coming to life! Stick THIS in your pipe and smoke it, Mr Parker! When was the last time *you* felt as arty and ALIVE as this?

Mr Parker's always banging on about *living*. Once he stood at the front of the class giving one of his know-all speeches about how much he loves it when he's cycling home from work and it's pouring rain and he's soaking wet with squelchy shoes because 'it makes him feel alive'. Teachers are massive freaks. I had to stop rolling my eyes halfway through that speech because I could hear Beth Wright sighing over at the desk next to me. Not a Parisian sigh, but a Greysworth sigh, like Mr Parker was a six-foot dollop of butterscotch Angel Delight. It's messed up. She'll probably be a teacher when she's older.

I've worked out that I like drawing women best. There's more *to* them for a start. More curves and bumpy, lumpy bits. I think that I'd like to pose as a life model one day. One day in the distant future, I mean, like when I'm *old* and don't care. Don't get me wrong, I like my body as it is now, but I like to appreciate it *alone*. It would feel very strange to jump right into letting a room full of strangers gawp at my bod before letting any one lad gawp at it in its glorious entirety first.

These life-drawing classes have taught me that there's so much I admire about women being comfy in their skin. It's just that sometimes it feels like everything, everywhere – on every bus shelter ad, in every aisle of Superdrug and in every stupid healthy Instagram trend – is telling us all to feel *uncomfortable* in our skin. I reckon being nice to your body is a form of rebellion. An act of civil disobedience.

Victor the life model has been stood in the same flipflop pose for a long time now. I guess this is how the French do it. So long that I'm overworking my drawing. The shading on the beard and the chest hair is too much. In my piece he looks like a yeti, which isn't a fair or realistic interpretation.

Then, oh no! Before our watchful eyes he faints and smacks the ground. The slap of his flesh on the worn wooden floors echoes around the shelves.

Everybody jumps up to help this poor naked man off the ground.

Suddenly it seems wildly inappropriate for a room of

us to be fully clothed and knocking back the vino while a naked man regains consciousness.

'Victor! Dear Victor! Give us a sign that you are still with us!' Mademoiselle Gigi fusses over him, unravelling her ginormous pashmina from round her neck to drape over his cold naked bod as he confirms that, yes, he's still alive.

'Well, there goes our model for the night . . .' Audrey shrugs before necking a recyclable cup of box wine.

'Ladies and gentlemen, I'm afraid we'll have to postpone the class!' Mademoiselle Gigi announces. It sounds like she's singing when she speaks. 'We cannot draw without a model, but we can, perhaps, stay here for the drinks!' She giggles. 'Oh! And, of course, make sure that dear Victor is all right. You'll be all right won't you, *mon cheri* . . .'

'I'll do it.' Blaine raises his hand and I swear to God, I almost tear it down myself. '*Moi?*' he offers, grinning. Lone handsome dimple ping-ping-pinging for all to see.

Is he serious? He'll step in for Victor?! No. Way. No. Effing. Way.

I notice a few of the artists look him up and down, sizing him up. They may as well get their paintbrushes at arm's length to be certain that they've got his proportions right. Oh God! He cannot be serious. He cannot be *naked*.

He'll just want it for the story. Just so he can show off by saying *Oh, yeah, I've been a life model a bunch of times. In Paris actually, yeah.* How pretentious! He is such a *poser*. The truest definition of the word. And I am *not* sticking around for this.

I jump up and out of my wooden chair. I start to gather my materials, quicker than I've ever moved in my entire life. I shove my pens in my bag and stick my sketchbook under my armpit.

'Where are you going?' he asks.

'Oh, get *over* yourself, Blaine!' As I swing round to leave, my bum knocks a jar of inky water over the *shhh* man who has been painting behind me.

It's all over his jumper and a bit of it has spilled onto his work. 'Oh my God, I'm so sorry! I – *Je suis désolé* – I – Blaine, stop threatening to take your knickers off and get me a tissue . . . please?'

Blaine starts laughing, and so do I, but I do my best to keep a straight face for the soggy jumper man. When Blaine reappears with a handful of paper towels he smiles at me and says, 'Your lips are purple, by the way.'

'So are yours. And your teeth are black.' It's the red wine. I'll have to remember that it does that.

They lifted Victor's legs up above his head to get the

blood flow circulating, which as you can imagine, is a very unpleasant thing to see in the nude. After he took a quiet moment sipping a glass of orange juice, our class resumed, with Victor – not Blaine (thank GOD) – doing simple sitting poses for the rest of the evening.

The fairy lights around the shop glow, and as I draw a close-up study of Victor's hands resting on the back of his chair, a few late-night customers peruse the shelves in the background. Audrey sits at the till, joining in with the class and drawing, ready to ring purchases through the register if anybody wants to buy anything. How cool is that? I wish we could bring Posers to Bennett's. I wonder if Greysworth could ever feel as dreamy as this?

'Pardon.' I snap out of my isn't-life-great haze when a bookshop wanderer asks to squeeze past me to get to a shelf.

I scoot my chair out of the way and I feel like this customer is really staring at my drawing. I subtly pull my sketchbook to my chest and realise that she's actually just staring at *me*.

What is it? My purple wine mouth? I purse my lips together to blend the stains into what hopefully looks like intentionally dark lipstick. She watches me and I look right back at her. She needn't think she can out-glare me.

I'm the reigning champ of all staring competitions (only counting the ones that are me vs my younger brother, but still). She's a smartly dressed woman, hair chopped into a very sharp black bob and she's wearing what looks like expensive statement jewellery. Huge plastic beads decorate her chest. She's wearing rectangular glasses with red frames and it feels like she's seeing right into my soul through the lenses. (I wish she'd tell me what my soul looks like if she's actually looking into it, because I have no idea and I've always wondered.)

I gulp like a cartoon character and wait for her to move past. Well, that was weird. I distractedly shade Victor's fingernails. What did she want? I watch her move around the bookshop. She's lurking among the shelves with a small bald man in a shiny suit. And for a spilt second I play the imaginary hair makeover game that I usually only do on Tony. It's totally involuntary; I obviously just can't help it any more. Mullets, mohawks and sideburns flash around his temples. It's best if you stay bald, bald guy. They make an odd couple, these two. They don't really seem like a couple. Or like bessie mates. They give off this weird baddie vibe and remind me of the skanky fox and cat in *Pinocchio* that keep hanging around corners before carting him off to the circus.

Are they planning on carting *me* off to the circus? Are they actually looking at me? Do they recognise me from the photos in the papers? Maybe I'm just being paranoid. Oh God, of course I'm paranoid. I don't know anybody in the city, and, really, nobody knows me, even if they know about that picture of me.

'*Merci beaucoup, Victor!* A round of applause for our valiant model!' Mademoiselle Gigi claps her hands together and slurs as she speaks, her purple lips twisting into a grin.

As everybody mingles around their drawings and paintings and I apologise again to the man whose jumper I splashed, Audrey rushes over to me with her phone.

I squint at the screen to see yet another news article about me with a candid shot of me on my hands and knees with the paper towels here tonight.

What the?

TABLOID TART

I yelp, nearly dropping the phone. I don't want it near me. How creepy! Who took that photo? I didn't see any paparazzi, but I guess that's their whole deal, hiding in bushes and invading people's privacy. Celeb privacy. But . . . why would they be papping me?! Was it that woman in the red glasses? I can't see where she is now; she must have left.

'What does it say, Audrey?!'

'It's unkind,' she warns. 'But it would roughly translate to something like . . . um . . . *BRIT BIMBO TRASHES PARIS'S BELOVED BOOKSHOP JUST HOURS AFTER CAUSING MAYHEM AT THE LOUVRE!*'

What?! How can they say that? Who even took that photo? I feel so creeped out by it. Also, I hardly trashed the place. I knocked some inky water over someone's painting and jumper. WITH MY BUM. I do not want to be known as the girl who trashed Paris with her bum.

'*Mon Dieu*. This is bad.' I sigh. A hard Parisian sigh.

'What's up?' Blaine waltzes over, pulling a cigarette from behind his ear and motioning for Audrey to lend him a lighter.

Get your own! Get a life! Get out of Paris – you've caused enough trouble.

'Paige is back in the press . . .' Audrey winces. 'And it's not good.'

She passes Blaine her phone and he frowns before saying, 'No way . . . is that *me* in the corner?! That's awesome.'

'This is serious, Blaine. The article is very negative. It totally underestimates Paige, and makes out that she's some foolish young girl causing problems for the city. It's not true.'

'It's not fair,' I add. 'Yes, you were in the photo too, Blaine, but I'm the one getting the headlines. Like it or not.'

'Yeah. Sorry, Paige. That does suck a bit . . . Audrey, could I borrow a light, please?'

The two of them weave their way through the wine-guzzling art crowd to smoke outside and I stay right here in Scowl City.

I know I can't blame this all on Blaine. Yes, he's a huge

stonking pain in the bum and I do feel like things wouldn't have got so out of hand if it wasn't for him . . . but at the same time I have to take some responsibility. It's not like I have no control over my actions. Even if sometimes it might feel like that in the moment. I'm a 'rebel girl', according to Audrey, and a 'woman', according to Mademoiselle Gigi. It's time I started thinking of myself in that way.

It wasn't me who plastered that drawing on the wall of the Louvre, but it was *my drawing*. And I feel misunderstood and I feel frustrated about whatever trash is written about me online, but if I keep trashing my work to myself and dismissing it as a 'stupid' drawing, then that makes it okay for other people to do that too.

I need to own it. I'm claiming ownership of this whole story. This is ridiculous, but it's also huge.

I mean, if the *stop looking at my tits* picture I made is really that 'dumb', then how has it proved to be so powerful? How is it news? And how has it got so many people this shook?

It's all dancing around in my head. Dancing around in gorilla masks.

What if that book Audrey showed me about the Guerilla Girls really is more relevant than I'd imagined? What if Blaine was actually on to something in the Louvre?

I look around this bookshop, at the sketches and paintings of Victor that we've all made tonight. They look great. Why can art in galleries only be created by certain people? Why should a drawing sketched in the Louvre be considered as 'causing mayhem'?

Why does it take something so small to rock the art world? Is it that fragile?

Maybe Mademoiselle Gigi is right, maybe I'm in exactly the right place at the right time and maybe this is me finding my path.

I should do something about this. I should do something.

A tap on my shoulder. 'Paige, are you okay?' It's Audrey, damp from the drizzly rain outside.

I nod. 'Yes. *Oui*.'

'Come along, Mademoiselle Gigi is about to recite some poetry; you have to see this!'

BÉBÉS TRISTES

Aujourd'hui I feel a little bit throbby around the temples.
I think last night's box wine and revelations must have
something to do with it. After a really luxurious lie in
with Simone the Cat keeping my feet warm, I've made
myself as presentable and chic as it's going to get. I haven't
drawn on any Audrey-style beauty spots, but I have put
red lipstick on and I'm determined not to let a drop of
vin rouge come within a millimetre of these smackers, so
that I can keep them this flawless all day.

I have a bit of time before it's my turn to cover the till
at Pages of Paris. I'm hoping a walk around this glorious
city will clear my head. I wave goodbye to Blaine who's
slumped over a battered old copy of *The Outsider* by
Albert Camus. He plays with his right earlobe as he reads.

'See ya.'

'Yeah, bye. Oh, Paige – hey, where are you off to?'

'I'm going to look for the Pompidou.'

'Cool. Try not to get chased out by guards this time, all right?' He smirks.

UGH.

'Whatever. Enjoy *The Outsider*, Blaine. I actually read it when I was thirteen; hope it's not too much of a challenge for you.'

I haven't actually read the entire thing. We just translated a passage from *L'Etranger* in a French lesson with Mrs McDonnell. I got the overall gist. It's enough to shut Blaine Henderson up for the rest of the afternoon, so it gets a five-star Good Reads rating from me.

I push through the old wooden doors and step out into the streets, the Pages of Paris bell pinging me goodbye. *Au revoir!* Heavy grey clouds loom above and – BUM – I realise I've left my umbrella in my room, but I'm not prepared to creep past Blaine to get it after that zinger, so I'll risk exploring without it.

I'm on my way to find one of Paris's most famous modern art galleries, the Pompidou Centre, or the Centre Pompidou as they call it here. There's a big illustrated diagram of it on my guidebook and apparently it's home to famous artworks by Duchamp, Matisse and Warhol. It'll be cool to see an Andy Warhol screen print in real life. I wonder if standing in front of the real thing will feel momentous and different to all the rip-off soup can prints you can buy in The Works amid the Banksy canvases and Live Laugh Love picture frames.

It's not long before I'm drawn to this city's tacky souvenir prints. I think that when it comes to holiday tat I sprout thick black wings and a nasty, pecky beak. I'm a total magpie for it. It turns out that Eiffel Tower keyrings and croissant-shaped magnets and coin purses that say I HEART PARIS are my Shiny Things.

Last time I was in a gift shop like this was in Skegton-On-Sea and Robbie the seaside fittie was the real keepsake I wished I was taking back to Greysworth with me . . . It feels a million miles away from here. I guess it pretty much is. I don't know the exact geographical measurement of the distance between us but seeing as I still haven't heard from him it's probably not important anyway.

What would happen if he's finally fixed his moped and he randomly picks this week to come and visit me in Greysworth, while I'm all the way over here? That would be just my luck.

But it could be oh so dreamy. I can see it now. He'd ride up to Bennett's, looking sharp in that baby blue Fred Perry shirt. He'd rev the engine of his scooter, declaring his undying love for me. Maybe he'd serenade me and offer to shower me with all the rock in Skegton-On-Sea (which would actually be quite painful come to think of it). Then Tony would march out onto the high street and tell him to bugger off.

Nothing ever came of my seaside romance with Robbie. Neither of us were very good at staying in touch. Texting him felt like a minefield, I ran out of things to say, and then I ran out of emojis to fall back on. It turns out that correspondence with a long lost fittie is much harder than it ever is with Holly or Mum. Time away from Robbie and time spent around Blaine is starting to convince me that boys are more trouble than they're worth.

'*Merci beaucoup!*' What a haul! That's a pink glittery Eiffel Tower snow globe for Holly (I defo want it for myself), a tea towel illustrated with every type of French cheese for my mum, and a pen in the shape of a baguette for Elliot. It has five different-coloured retractable nibs. He'll think it's the dog's bollocks. *Les couilles des chiens!*

As I walk along the road, away from the *Mona Lisa* dabbing T-shirts, in what I think is the direction of the art gallery, huge raindrops begin to splat all over the pavement. Before I know it, the sky has opened up and it begins to chuck it down.

Crap. I squint up at the name of the street. Impasse Berthaud. I'm not sure where I am in relation to the Pompidou.

That's when I see it. A small street sign that says MUSÉE DE LA POUPÉE. That means doll museum; it's a sign for a doll museum. Wow!

Now I know this might not be on the sparkly list of highbrow cultural must-sees for university admissions staff to read about, but I can't resist. My feet take me there in the rain.

The path leads me along a quiet alley, away from the hustle and bustle, through these dramatic iron gates. It kind of feels like it's somewhere I'm not sure if I'm allowed into. I push the door open and it feels very dark and very quiet.

I walk into a room lined with long glass cabinets. The displays are rammed, chockablocked, stuffed full of dolls. Babies of all sizes, made of rubber and plastic and porcelain, squash into wooden cots and prams and highchairs. There are ones with little knitted bonnets and others that are all done up in weird traditional national costumes. There are tiny little ceramic women with golden ringlets and velvet petticoats who perch inside very fancy ornate doll's houses that must have belonged to the kind of kids that *The Secret Garden* was written about. It feels a bit like I've just accidentally wandered into an old children's book. The kind we keep under Children's Classics at Bennett's in Greysworth for grandparents who come sniffing for Christmas presents in an attempt to 'get the little beggars away from screens'. The only sound in this place is coming from an old grandfather clock that is tick-tocking away and feels totally enchanted.

I seem to be the only living, moving being with opposable thumbs in here, but I'm being watched by hundreds of little eyes. Some are painted onto wax or papier-mâché faces, while some are made of glass. Imagine all the things they've seen, all the children they've comforted, all the playgrounds they've been lost and found in. Some of them are centuries old and a fair few of them look proper mank and scary to be honest, but I still like them.

I move through the small strip-lighted galleries, marvelling at the curious little faces behind the glass. I've never seen a collection like this; there's nothing like this back at home. Jenny Matthews had the most toys I'd ever seen when we were in Year Three. She even had the Sylvanian Families barge *and* the post office, but this place tops that. Even if it's not on Lonely Planet's top itineraries for art lovers, I feel like I've stumbled on a total gem.

I'm not a kid any more; I'm about to start the rest of

my life. I wonder if anyone goes to uni clutching their fave childhood teddies or if anybody takes their old Baby Born along to freshers' week. Being around all this stuff, especially the display case filled with Barbies and Polly Pockets, makes me feel a big pang of nostalgia. It makes me feel like being small again without any worries about money or my future or messages from boys, which would be quite nice. I've spent sixteen years desperate to get away from Greysworth and now that I'm on the brink of moving it feels a bit daunting.

I read a small handwritten plaque on one of the displays. It says that Balzac actually used to keep a doll's house filled with little dolls on his desk to help him come up with fictional characters for his books. I guess they're not just for children after all. I'm staring at a cabinet of crying babies – aka *bébés tristes* – thinking how creepy it is to be a little kid playing with a doll who permanently has a face like a slapped bum, and how it's through playing with plastic babies that we are taught how to care and nurture from a really young age and that that's great and everything but it also raises a load of questions about society's expectations for girls; it means that we learn how to soothe and look after a permanently miserable goblin and what space does that leave for girls to be the unhappy, slapped-bum-faced ones? There is no space for that, like there's no space for women in galleries unless their boobs are hanging out of their flimsy gowns . . .

'*Excusez-moi, mademoiselle, nous fermerons bientôt.*'

WHOA!

I think I heard somebody scream, and I think that somebody was me.

'What?! Sorry! Oh, *pardon*. You scared me!' I'm all flustered. I feel like I've been caught sifting through someone else's bag, and instead of hairbrushes, loose change and tampons they've got a massive collection of weird dolls squashed in there.

Duh, of course someone is working here. I shouldn't be this shocked, although the fact I hadn't seen or heard any sign of life made me think that maybe the life-size dolls in sailor suits waddle out of their high chairs and lock up at the end of their shift.

The museum lady blinks at me. She looks a bit like a doll herself, a grandma doll. The lines folding around her pale eyes are so delicate and symmetrical that they look as if they could have been perfectly painted on by a very skilled and steady-handed Geppetto in a workshop.

'We close now.'

'Oh, okay. I'm sorry I didn't realise the time –'

'It is your first visit to the museum?' she asks.

I nod. 'Yes, thank you. I just found it by chance. I'm so happy that I did.' I look around at the cabinets, mentally waving goodbye to them. So long, baby freaks.

'*Bon*. You like it?'

'*Oui, oui!* It's magical.'

'We've been here for a long time; some of these dolls are very old. They make me feel like a *jeune fille*.' She waves me along a corridor, motioning for me to follow her and I do. 'I'll take you out this way.'

This is when I notice her peculiar little outfit. She's wearing a white lab coat with the Musée de la Poupée logo embroidered on gold thread across the shoulders. Think Hell's Angels but cute. And a bit weird. Like somebody's got crafty on one of the fetching things we have to wear in the science lab at school when we're dicking around with Bunsen burners or those mini light bulbs.

'*Bonne nuit.*' She says goodnight to the dolls before turning off the light and closing the door behind us. I am so grateful that she found me before shutting me in there. Thank GOD. I'd transform into a toy version of myself, never seeing my mum again. Holly would have to tap on the glass to tell me about the latest developments in her relationship with Jamie.

'I say hello and goodbye to the dolls every day. They are nice people to work with. Good listeners.' She laughs as we enter what seems to be some kind of workshop.

'Wow.' This is astonishing. Even more so than everything I've just seen.

L'Hôpital des Poupées. Before me is a room that looks like a garage, but instead of being filled with mechanical tools, it is packed with doll parts. Shelves and shelves of chubby plastic arms and dislocated legs with little red-leather T-bar sandals on their feet stack up on top of each other. There's an operating table piled high with mangled dolly torsos and frayed teddy bears. And, of course, a wall of decapitated heads, some with eyes, some without.

'I'm a doll doctor. I fix broken toys.'

That explains the white coat, I think to myself. A paint-splattered radio with a big old-fashioned antenna plays fuzzy big band numbers and the babies look like they'd probably like to dance if they only could.

'Incredible.'

I peer at the tins of paints and varnishes, at the pots of paintbrushes, some so fine that they must be used to pick out the teeny-weeniest details. She's not a doll doctor; she's an artist. This place is a masterpiece. This deserves to be seen by the world and hit the national press.

'My father always wanted a son, you see. He trained me to be an electrician and that's how I started my career, fixing machines. I didn't really have dolls when I was growing up, but one day somebody gave me a broken porcelain *bébé* to fix and it turned out that I was, in fact, very good at it. My hands are as steady as the Seine.' She holds her still, miniature doll-like hands out to demonstrate.

'I think you're amazing.'

'It's just what I do.' She shrugs. 'I keep childhood alive. Those are the happiest days of your life.'

I've heard a few adults say that before and quite frankly . . . it seems like it's all downhill from here if living my best life has already been wasted on SATs and peeling dried PVA glue off my hands.

'*D'accord*, I must be getting on,' she says, ushering me out of the door.

It feels very strange stepping back out onto the streets of Le Marais after being in that dream world. Everything suddenly seems so loud and fast. Mopeds rev past me and tiny curly dogs on leads bark at each other without their owners even noticing. Women kiss each other on the cheeks and a bar across the road pumps out a cheesy Eurovision-worthy techno beat. Time flies when you're having an existentialist moment in a doll museum. I don't know, maybe it was that *Tom's Midnight Garden* style clock, but somehow I lost all track of time in there. There's no way I'll get around the Pompidou before work now; I've left it too late. Better dash back to Pages of Paris before the next downpour.

CRYSTAL MAZE

I don't know how the Tumbleweeds back in Margot's day would have managed to get through a whole book each day as Mademoiselle Gigi said they did. Maybe I'm just a slow reader, but I'm still on *The Woman Destroyed* and, granted, it might be taking me slightly longer to finish as I'm discussing each chapter at length with Simone de Beauvoir's feline reincarnation, Simone the Cat.

The shop is buzzing with customers.

Second-hand book collectors check inside old dusty hardbacks to see if they're rare editions, while somebody asks if they can leave flyers for a local yoga class by the till. A man sits cross-legged in the chair by the typewriter, reading a newspaper and sipping a Baudelaire coffee from the cafe. There are book blogger girls staging perfect photos of each other amid the shelves, books piled up in their arms, and a happy toddler in a pushchair babbles in baby language to the cat (maybe he's also reading some feminist existentialist theory).

Pages of Paris, much like the Musée de la Poupée, is here because people care about it enough to keep it going. It's a cause. Everybody in here, customers and volunteers, is fighting for that cause in their own way.

Behind where I sit at the counter, there's a door that says STAFF ONLY on it. It's the office. While I have a quiet moment between anybody wanting to pay for things, I slip behind the scenes to snoop around.

This office would have been Margot's HQ when she was running things. Right now, it's a mess. Have you ever seen that old game show *The Crystal Maze*? It's on the Challenge channel all the time. There's a bit in every episode where the contestants stand inside a dome filled with gold and silver tokens flying around it and they have to grab as many as they can. Well, it looks a bit like this but it's old papers. Receipt books and order forms dating back to God knows when. Catalogues and old ledgers and photographs.

It makes Tony's office in the old pre-makeover branch of Bennett's look as glam as a Hollywood dressing room. And that's really saying something because Adam told me about the time Tony complained that maggots kept landing on his desk. He had no idea what was going on. It happened again and again until one day a dead pigeon fell through one of the polystyrene ceiling tiles and crashed onto his keyboard in a mass of rotting feathers and mush. How gross is that?

I sift through box files and folders of I don't know what, keeping my eyes peeled for something in particular.

'Paige, a customer is looking for a copy of Greta Thunberg's book . . .' Blaine stands in the doorway.

'*No One Is Too Small to Make a Difference?*' I get in there with the title. So full of myself. I'm a walking, talking bookselling genius with an encyclopaedic knowledge.

'That's the one!' a gentleman calls from over Blaine's shoulder. 'I knew it was something along those lines! Do you have it?'

I clamber towards the till, out of this cave filled with old stationery and other people's memories. 'I'm sure I've seen it. It should be with our books about climate activism, just over that way.' He follows my pointy hand directions.

'What are you doing in here?' Blaine asks, looking around the office.

'Last night at life drawing, Mademoiselle Gigi told me about these sort of autobiographical accounts Margot used to make all her visitors write on the old typewriter in exchange for staying here. I'd love to find Gigi's diary entry from when she was young. I'm thinking it's got to be buried in here somewhere, right? Nobody seems to have thrown anything away . . .'

BOYS IN ROOMS

After we shut up the shop downstairs for the night, ushering the last loved-up stragglers onto the streets and selling the last dog-eared second-hand copy of *Brave New World* from the shelves, Audrey announced that she was off to meet her ex again. She'd scraped her dark hair back into a slick bun and gelled a perfect little curl in the middle of her forehead for the occasion. She looked like a film star from the silent era or something.

'Stay out of trouble, Mademoiselle Turner.' She winked at me as she stomped away from Pages of Paris and into the night.

It was all mine. A shiny, perfect evening in Paris all to myself. It struck me like a bolt of lightning that I could do whatever I felt like. That if I'm really here (and I've pinched myself enough times to know for sure now), then I'm throwing myself into living my best sophisticated Parisian life. Your childhood years can't actually be the best days of your life – not if you've lived them in Greysworth and it's taken sixteen long years to get anywhere as beautiful and fascinating as Paris.

So I made sure I had my umbrella on me this time, and then I walked along little streets and huge grand avenues that I hadn't seen before. I took photos of Metro signs and shopfronts and churches with gargoyles spilling out of the stone, and I sat by myself in a brasserie and ordered the most delicious crème brûlée known to (wo)man. It was nothing like the ones you buy in a six-pack from Tesco's back home. It was crunchy and oozy, and I honestly think I may have had an out-of-body experience somewhere around the second or third mouthful.

I called Mum to tell her about the dreamy brûlée and Pages of Paris and the doll museum, and when she asked me if I had enough money I lied and said yes, even though I could feel my cheeks prickle and burn with the shame that I'd, in fact, lost it within hours of arriving here. It was strange to think of her sitting on the sofa in her sofa-spot that neither me or Elliot are allowed on* back in Greysworth. (*My designated bum dent is on the other end of the sofa and Elliot usually lies on the floor to watch telly.) In those four walls with all the familiar school photos and cushions and TV guides, while I was here, squinting to see exactly which building the Eiffel Tower was poking out of in the skyline, like some spotty lad photobombing a pic of two friends in an under-eighteens nightclub on Gold Street.

When it started to rain again I decided there was a definite line between looking chic in an *Umbrellas of Cherbourg* kind of way, and looking anti-chic in an Umbrellas of Poundland That Have Had It kind of way, and I had definitely crossed that line.

That's when I came back here, to my room above the shop, and got changed into my pyjamas. Sad-That-I'm-Not-Even-Sad-About-It Confession: getting home and changing into my comfies is my favourite part of the day. I'm dry, I've reached my snuggly loungewear peak and decide that with the room all to myself I'm just going to use this opportunity to fully explore the books crammed into these four walls.

A knock on the bedroom door. Oh God. What is it? Who is it?

'*Oui?* Um, hello?!' I call out.

'Hello. It's me. It's Blaine.'

Really?! I look up at the ceiling and whisper '*Pourquoi?!*'

in despair. That means *why*, by the way.

I open the door just a fraction and stick my head in the gap so that he can't see the extreme comfiness going on from the chin down.

'I think she wants to join you. She was purring at your door.'

Simone scampers through my legs and makes *herself* comfy on my bed.

'Oh. All right,' is all I can muster.

I didn't know he was the Cat Whisperer.

'What are you doing?' he asks, blue eyes wide in the dark corridor.

'Me? Oh, I just got in. I'm just going to read actually.'

'Cool. Cool. I think your room has the most books in it by far.'

'Yeah . . . so that's me sorted for the night.' I nod. 'What have you been up to?'

'Oh, when we closed I just took my camera out, shot a few cool things. But it's raining now so I'm back.'

'Well, then . . . have a good night . . .' I turn on my heels, closing the door on Blaine when something darts across my toes and I SCREAM IN SHOCK.

'What's wrong?! Why are we shouting?!' Blaine howls, obviously freaked out by my shrieking.

'MOUSE! MOUSE ON MY FOOT!'

I flung the door open somewhere between being stampeded on by the rodent and jumping to my bed for safety, so now Blaine is in here and there is no way of hiding the pyjama truth from him any longer.

'Where did it go?' he asks, scanning the room for nasty little intruders.

'I don't know!' I hug my knees to my chest. The mouse protection position has been assumed.

'So this explains why Simone wanted to get in here then, doesn't it?' Blaine's lips curl into a smile and he goes all gooey-eyed, stroking her furry feline belly as she rolls on the old wooden floorboards. It looks like a shot from one of those cheesy Hot Guys with Cats calendars. It's a living nightmare.

'Yeah, sure. *Nice one*, Simone. Thanks for giving that rat a good seeing to; you really had my back. I owe you one. *NOT*.'

Blaine laughs. And he should, because I'm funny. 'Wait, you're not scared of mice are you, Paige?'

'Yes! Well . . . I just don't like how fast they move and how you can't see where they've gone – *OHMYGODTHEREITIS*!'

Blaine yelps, like actually *yelps*, as the mouse zooms

across the room, past Simone (who obviously couldn't give a flying flip about it), and he jumps onto the end of *my* bed. I don't know what's more alarming: the fact that I'm staying in a pest-infested room, or the fact that the number-one king of the art-school sulky boy pests has just plonked his bony backside on my bed.

GIRLS IN TEARS

I was pretty certain that I, Mademoiselle Turner, *would* stay out of trouble this evening, and I'm not sure how having Blaine Henderson in my room fits in with that.

'At least it's gone now.' He exhales, stretching his long gangly legs out ahead of him while making himself at home at the other end of my bed. The ancient springs squeak under the weight of our awkward bodies. Not that Blaine looks awkward. He's the definition of 'chillaxed' right now, while I perch here, arms folded across my PJ-clad chest.

'Did it actually leave the room?' I ask. 'It was hard to tell with all your crying going on TBH. It looks like I'm not the only one who's afraid of mice.'

'Oh my God, you *saw* how quickly that thing ran!' His eyebrows disappear all the way up under his floppy curly fringe.

It's very strange. Having a boy in my room. Someone who isn't my brother and hasn't come in here with the intention of showing me how to eat Penguin or Viscount biscuits layer by layer.

The Parisian rain is trickling down the Parisian window, and I'm here, in Paris, with Blaine and we're living in a bookshop. A fairy-tale bookshop.

This is mad and insane and pretty much what I'd been saving up all my emotional pocket money for last summer before I knew what a total sod Blaine was. Or should I say, what a total sod he *is*? What is he? Why am I even giving him the opportunity to deliver this monologue about the book he's reading?

I've lost my bed to a cat and a boy with an earring.

And I'm in my pyjamas.

It's not like he hasn't seen them strewn over the cobbled streets already. But I just don't know if this is decent. I'm not wearing a bra, so my arms will remain folded across my chest for the duration of this visit. There's a hole in my pyjama bottoms somewhere around the inner thigh so my legs will also remain crossed. It doesn't take a body language expert to tell you that I'm not a hundred per cent pleased with my wardrobe choice. This isn't how I imagined I'd be dressed when entertaining male company in my (mouse-infested) boudoir.

He's just sitting on the end of my bed like he's Holly or something. If he was actually Holly, then he'd actually be lying on his belly and asking whether I think he should grow his fringe out rather than going on and on about those books by the serious Norwegian bloke with the big grey beard.

'Honestly, everybody needs to read Knausgård . . .'

I don't think he's even noticed that I'm not into what he's chatting on about. Where are the mice at now? I knew I should have stuck at paying the recorder; if I could play a tune and muster up some of that Pied Piper magic to make them dance their way out of their grotty little hiding places and scare Blaine Henderson out of my room to end his BORING 'all the books I read are by really clever guys' routine, then I would.

All of a sudden Audrey thunders into the room. She's wet, soaking, like she didn't take an umbrella out with her, and her make-up has gone all streaky down her cheeks like a clown from a horror film.

'Hey, Audrey!' I chime, happy for her to break the monotony of Blaine's bore-off book review and embarrassed in case she thinks we were actually canoodling in here while she was away. Not that anyone who uses the term 'canoodling' would ever get the chance to canoodle in the first place. *Mon Dieu*, what's wrong with me?

'Sorry, I don't want to interrupt.' She slumps onto her bed and goes about unzipping her big clumpy boots and kicking them off.

'I must sleep. Blaine, please go.'

So that is how it's done. Mentally noted and underlined three times for emphasis. Please go. Is there anything I won't learn from Audrey?

'Same.' I fake-yawn. 'I'd better be hitting the hay now too. Long day.' I even throw in a sleepy stretch, as I'm so committed to my Bafta-Winning Role as Tired Girl No. 2.

'Oh, are you going to bed? I didn't realise those were pyjamas . . .' He nods towards my ensemble. Great. Fabulous.

I make myself mentally stay behind after class and write up one thousand imaginary lines that say 'He's just self-centred; that is not a reflection on your day-to-day banging wardrobe choices.'

'All right then, I'll see you tomorrow. Goodnight, Paige.'

I wait for the door to close and for the footsteps to creak away down the corridor before hissing, 'Audrey, I'm not actually tired! I just wanted him to get out because he was going on and on about how this bloke who's written a load of books about his "struggle" is the greatest writer to have ever lived and it was such a major eye-roll . . .' I expect her to snigger along with that, but she doesn't.

'And *I've* actually been thinking about something,' I continue, '. . . a plan . . . to do with the whole big gallery drama the other day that I wanted to run by you . . .'

She's much nicer to me than she is to Blaine. More polite – maybe she thinks I'm too wussy for the full Audrey experience shebang. 'Paige, do you mind if we turn out the light, so we can sleep? I just need to close my eyes and rest.'

Well, this is the downside to being roomies, I guess. If I had my way, I'd stay up all night reading these books until I'm too tired to be afraid of secret mice raves that happen in the dark.

I slide into bed and pull the blankets over my legs.

'Sure, I guess it is pretty late. And we have work tomorrow. But we're at work so at least we don't have to get up really early or anything. Just early enough to fit in a bit of breakfast. *Petit déjeuner* . . .'

She switches the lights off and plunges us into darkness. I think I was talking too much. Okay then, that's that.

Lights off. It's just me and Audrey. Her bed is on the

other side of the room and this is the first night she's been in here for bedtime. It's silent. What should I say?

'How was your night?'

'Um. It was fine.'

'Goodnight!' I call out into the dark, sounding way too awake, like I'm singing or something.

'Night,' she says in return.

No one can see if you twiddle your thumbs in the dark. Which is just as well.

Whenever I've stayed at Holly's or when we've had big group sleepovers for birthdays with people from school it's never awkward like this. Usually I don't even remember falling asleep. We just end up exhausted after a night of hysterical singing and pigging out.

I can hear Audrey sniffing in the dark. Is she crying?

Cool Audrey? Audrey the wolf, who always knows what to do and say? Crying? And she's stuck in here with me. God, this is awkward.

Or maybe she just has allergies, in which case sharing a room with a cat as old and furry as Simone is way more problematic than sharing a room with me.

A little whimper escapes through the pitch-black darkness of our bookshelf bedroom.

'Audrey?' My voice feels massive, even though I'm trying

to whisper, unsure of whether I can actually trust what I think I'm hearing.

She doesn't answer at first; there's just a long massive pause, which makes me worry for a sec that I've, in fact, been listening to the evil ghostly spirit of the long-gone bookshop owner, Margot, crying. Then Audrey clears her throat and says, 'Yes?'

'Are you okay?' I shine the torch on my phone at her way too prematurely (mainly to rule out the possibility of the ghost) and she screams as I catch her smudged eyeliner and blotchy tear-stained cheeks. 'God! What are you doing?!' she wails.

I shove my phone under my pillow, killing the light under a big feathery lump of orange paisley. 'Sorry.'

After a while I ask, 'What's wrong?'

'It's stupid.' She sniffs. 'It's just boy stuff . . .'

'Well, in my limited experience, boy stuff always feels stupid . . . but it never really is,' I offer, and listen to her hard-as-nails heart break.

And in this dark room I feel like I'm seeing a totally different Audrey for the first time.

I'm not being funny, Paige, but I'm sending you this postcard (depicting some old 1960s shopping precinct that I had no idea ever existed in Greysworth???) to tell you that things are getting p-retty weird here at Bennett's without you . . . Honestly, I actually think Tony MISSES YOU. Seriously. I caught him reading your list of Funny Customer Names and he looked like he was getting tearful. To be fair, he could have just been crying over Chris Peacock. Truth is, I'm still not over that. ALSO: LOVE is in the AIR. And, no, it's not the Ambi Pur plug-ins Nikki bought. I think there's something blossoming between Adam and Parisian Sabine. They've been speaking in very hushed tones over their packed lunches to each other in the staffroom. STEAMY! Anyway, I hope you're having the best time, making sure you've hit EVERY SIGHT in your guidebook, and snogged every fit *garçon* in Paris! Lots of love, Holly XXXX

FURRY LITTLE LEGEND

Amid the shelves at Pages of Paris.

You can just sense it when a customer wants to speak to you. They don't always just SAY. Sometimes they'll sigh. That really bugs me. I deliberately don't answer to dramatic-everybody-pay-me-attention sighs. Sometimes if they're shopping with someone else they might make a big deal out of saying 'WELL, MAYBE WE SHOULD ASK SOMEBODY WHO WORKS HERE,' when you're stood so nearby that there is really no excuse for such nuttery. Nuttery. That's a term I just made up specifically for this kind of behaviour.

It's that woman. The one with the glasses who brushed past me at life drawing. But she's wearing different glasses this time. These frames are small and rectangular with funky lilac lenses. I wonder if she has a whole wardrobe of different glasses for multiple occasions.

Staring-into-Paige-Turner's-soul glasses. Freaking-Paige-Turner-out-at-work sunglasses. Two for the price of one at Specsavers. Terms and conditions apply; hurry while stocks last.

This woman, she's hovering. I'm not saying I'm a psychic or that I can see what other people are up to at all times or anything, but I don't really believe that a second-hand copy of the *Winter European Timetable 2008* can be that interesting to any living soul. What's she doing with it? I feel like she's pretending to look at it when really she's just using it as an excuse to look at me again.

It's freaking me out. Is she a reporter? Is *she* the person who printed the piece about me trashing Paris with my bum?

Am I just being paranoid? Totally. Surely there's no conspiratorial explanation for her being here. She's just a woman, minding her own beeswax, and she likes train timetables. Old ones.

I glance at her from the corner of my eye and she opens her mouth as if she's about to say something to me –

'Paige?'

Blaine pokes his head round the bookshelf behind me and I don't just jump out of my skin – I somersault all the way out of it like a *Britain's Got Talent* finalist.

'Ah! Yes! What? How can I help?' I don't know why I just said that to Blaine. He caught me off guard and in the middle of some scary espionage-y fantasy about being followed by this woman.

'Is there, like, a box of tissues or something?'

'Um. I don't know?' I shrug, aware that the lurker is still just a few steps away from me. If she *is* a pap and she's listening in, what hot Paige Turner scoop is she going to get me on this time? Stupid Greysworth Teen Has Used All The Tissues In Paris To Blow Her Big Gallery-Ruining Nose?!

'How would I know? Why?'

'Simone's had an accident. There's cat pee everywhere.'

Actually, I've never been so grateful to be interrupted by an incontinent cat. Thanks, Simone, you furry little legend. You may have just saved me from another front-page scandal.

I'm on that stinky scene faster than you can say *sacré bleu*!

While I'm on my hands and knees scrubbing the floor, I watch the woman in the glasses leave. She didn't even bother buying the train timetable. So what's her deal?

Hey, I'm sure that while Pages of Paris feels worlds away from Bennett's in Greysworth, it probably still attracts some freaky customers. There's a regular back home who I always catch sneezing inside books from the Natural History section. She does it every time. Big, dramatic wet sneezes, with the books held open right in front of her face. It's really weird. And disgusting. What do you say? *Can you stop doing that?* No one can really stop a sneeze, can they, but they can carry tissues if they're that prone to doing it. I don't know her name, she doesn't have a loyalty card, and I've never actually seen her buy anything.

Maybe the chick with the glasses is this shop's equivalent. But less snotty.

'What are you doing on the floor, Paige?' Audrey stands above me, looking concerned. Today she's wearing a beautiful pink silk kimono, with a studded leather belt and tall black platform boots.

'Oh, just cleaning up after Simone.' My knees click as I scoop the wet paper towels up.

'Ew. Well, I hope that doesn't put you off this.' She holds a little box from the patisserie under my nose and it smells divine.

She smiles. 'I wanted to say thank you for last night. You made me feel much better about everything with my ex. It's so nice to have a friend here.'

'Oh, Audrey . . . thank you!' I go to hug her before

remembering I'm clutching a handful of pissy tissues. 'Let me wash my hands first, okay?'

The two of us cotch on the old leather sofa by the shop's coffee machine. I tuck into the *tarte au fraises* Audrey's treated me to. It's delicious.

'I still can't believe CCTV footage of YOUR FACE in the Louvre is doing the rounds online and in the newspapers,' Audrey laughs, holding her phone to show me the latest internet think piece on it.

'It's crazy. They're calling me "*la fille au chapeau*" – the girl in the hat.'

It really goes to show that one fashion statement can haunt you your whole life. It's just as well I hadn't accidentally taken the art world by storm in something *really* embarrassing, like the nightie I've had since I was nine. I still wear it, seeing as it's so misshapen and tattered it still fits. What would they call me if I'd been running around the Louvre in that?!

'I've been thinking, Audrey, all of this negative media attention makes me want to do something about it.'

'What do you want to do?'

'Well, what if we *gave* them something to write about? What if a group of us actually gave them something to look at?!'

It pains me to say it. I mean, like, it physically hurts. That watery-eye feeling you get when you pluck a stray hair out of the monobrow territory. Like, OUCH, it's torture, but it's necessary . . . That's a lot like how it feels to say that Blaine Henderson may, in fact, be a genius.

Well, I immediately want to take that back and clarify.

I glance at him across the shop. He's pouting in the shop window, checking out his reflection and doing that thing men on the Gillette razor adverts do, stroking their face and thinking about how handsome they look. Granted, he doesn't look like a genius.

'When Blaine stuck my drawing on the wall at the Louvre I don't think he did it to be "subversive" or kick this whole thing off . . . but what if we did it again? What if a group of us got together . . . I don't know, maybe some of the life-drawing class people might want to take part . . . What if we all showed up at different galleries around Paris and we all stuck our own work on the walls . . . ?'

'Right . . .' Audrey nods, looking very serious. She gets up and begins pacing back and forth in front of me.

I nibble at the last remaining crumbs of my friendship *tarte*, watching her think things through, mumbling a few words to herself in French and then shaking her fist and laughing. 'Yes, Paige! This is a great idea. I like this idea!'

'Phew! Great! I'm glad you think so.'

'We spread the word; we invite people. I know many people who will love this!' she says excitedly. 'And when we gather at the museums we form a grass-roots, anti-establishment collective . . .'

'As an act of peaceful protest,' I continue. 'We're not disrespecting the art or the institution, we're merely challenging the idea that art can only be created by certain people in a certain way.'

'Well, when do we do this?' Audrey asks.

'We don't have much time. I'm going home at the end of the week.'

'*Without further ado!*' Audrey laughs. 'We have to come up with a plan!'

'*Vive la révolution!*'

'We need more coffee for this.' She starts banging around on the old espresso machine, while I make lists and brainstorms. Which galleries do we want to go to and where will we have the most impact?

If we come up with ways to share it on social media, then we can invite people to come along and join in. All they will need to take part is a pencil. If we can coordinate exactly when and where we'll be, then it'll be a bit like a flash mob when everybody turns up and gets drawing. A flash mob without the marriage proposals and show tunes.

'I guess I'll wear my *chapeau* again!' I offer.

'Yes!' Audrey chimes. 'We should all wear hats when we go to the museums! Like the Guerilla Girls and their masks!'

I beam. 'Cool! You'll wear berets too?!'

'Paige. C'mon, really. Not all French people wear berets.'

'Oh God, no. Sorry. That was stupid.' *Duuuuuuuh.*

VIVE
LA RÉVOLUTION

My alarm wakes me up. Today's the big day and Audrey is already up.

She sits across the bedroom, wearing a bright red jumpsuit and a knitted balaclava with the face cut out. Before I can rub the sleep from my eyes I nearly scream. She looks awesome once you get over the initial WTF-ery of it all.

'Paige. Comrade. We've taken the decision to shut the shop today to support the gallery occupation,' she says, dead pleased with herself.

'OMG, really? Is that okay with everyone? I mean, it's amazing and if everyone's on board then I'm over the moon –'

'It's what Margot would have wanted,' she says, nodding, hand on her heart.

I jump out of bed. We've got some demonstrating to do! I scrabble around through my clothes for something to wear. Audrey has inspired me to go for A Look. While I don't have anything red or jumpsuity or balaclavish, I decide that wearing all black makes me feel tough. Doc Martens, opaque tights, black pinafore . . . and I watch myself in the mirror as I put the vintage beret on top of my head.

We gather outside the front of the shop and hang a sign in the window. There's a good turnout. It turns out that Audrey really does know a lot of people who are willing to join the cause. I recognise some of them from the gig we went to. It's not like it was at the gig. I don't feel awkward or out of place. I feel like I'm in exactly the right place at the right time. I'm not a slimy tadpole-y newt thing; I'm a big glistening toad. Marcel introduces me to the women from the feminist book club. They tell me they're thrilled to be involved, and they've even brought a banner along with them. It's rolled up now but looks pretty cool.

The air is crispy and cold, and the sun is shining.

'Bit chilly, innit?' Paul shiver-dances next to me, pulling the zip on his grey hoodie to reveal a home-made protest T-shirt. 'Check it out!'

It says STOP LOOKING AT MY TITS in big letters.

'That's incredible! I love it!'

'Paul! We were supposed to wait until we were in the gallery to show Paige these!' Johnny slaps him on the wrist.

'Oh, I couldn't help it!' Paul chuckles, pulling his zip up to his chin.

'Do you have one on too, Johnny?' I ask, impressed beyond belief.

'Shhhh!' He flashes his own T-shirt from under his sweater, the letters stretching over his large belly.

Carlos pulls the shutters closed on the shop, locking up for the day. He smooths gaffer tape round the edges of a paper sign, sealing it up there for everyone to see. In French and English it says:

IN AN ACT OF SOLIDARITY PAGES OF PARIS WILL BE
SITTING IN AND DRAWING AS A PROTEST AT THE
MUSÉE D'ORSAY AT 12 NOON. IF YOU'D LIKE TO JOIN THE
CAUSE, THEN BRING PAPER AND A PENCIL TO THE MUSEUM
AND LOOK OUT FOR LES FILLES AUX CHAPEAUX.

'Remember what I said? This shop belongs to us all,' Audrey reminds me, a vision in red.

'I'm no good at drawing,' says Luc, 'but I could write a poem about it!'

'YES! This is a bohemian uprising!' Mademoiselle Gigi laughs. 'Let's show them what we can do!'

MUSÉE D'ORSAY

We walk along the Left Bank by the River Seine. I think about the Musée de la Poupée doll doctor's hands, steady like the green water that runs beside us, twinkling in the sunlight. I can feel this fizzy sensation rising in my chest. I don't mean the kind of fizz you get after downing a can of Pepsi really hard. No, it's way better than that. It's happy. I feel like I'm living in a film. Don't ask who would play me in the silver-screen version of my life, I have no idea. But if this was a film, this is the bit where me and my gang of rebels would walk side by side in slow motion – my character would have no trouble seeing through these vintage shades – and one of the songs from Holly's French babes playlist would provide the soundtrack. Oh! And my money's on it being that Bunny and Clyde song – that would be so perfect right now.

We pass a row of bookstalls on the riverbank. The shelves fold out of these little metal cabin things that look so old they must have been here for ever. I wonder what it's like to work here. Maybe one day I'll have my own little folding bookshop right in this spot. I'd only sell books I like. All of those freaks from Greysworth who ask for books about chatting up women or making clothes out of dog hair could bother some other poor bookseller with a less cool shop.

Ooooh, it's an old French edition of *Madeline* by Ludwig Bemelmans! I could go mad here. Mentally I'm piling old books from this tiny stall under my armpits, but realistically I know I can't spend everything I have in my bank account here; they're called *savings* for a reason. But *Madeline* . . . it's set in Paris and I am *in* Paris and I want it. And Madeline is one of the original mouthy little madams. She's always getting into scrapes and coming out on top. I think she'd handle being slammed on the cover of a national newspaper pretty well.

'Sorry, everyone . . . *Je suis désolé!* I'll just buy this . . . really quickly. *Tout de suite!* Then it's straight back to the rebellion . . . !'

I don't know if anything has ever made me as happy as I am in this moment. Skipping along the Seine, on my way to an art gallery I've always wanted to visit, with a group of fascinating booklovers, with a new old book under my arm. It makes me feel less nervous about what we're about to do.

This is what Audrey was talking about. Being part of a collective feels great. We have each other's backs. I don't feel alone. Strength in numbers to make a change. Even Blaine isn't getting on my nerves as he rolls a cigarette between his fingers, large sketchbook folded under his arm. It's a Parisian miracle.

'Wow.'

We stand, stunned, side by side in the entrance to the museum.

It's a huge hall filled with white marble sculptures and paintings in massive gilded frames. There's a HA-UGE fancy clock at the end of the room. As daylight pours through the curved glass ceiling, this place takes my breath away. It's more beautiful than anywhere I've ever been before.

'Can you believe this used to be a train station?' I whisper. Thinking of all the people who must have dashed through here to catch a train, using THAT crazy clock to make it on time.

'It has nothing on Greysworth Central . . .' Blaine shoots me a side-eye and laughs.

'Okay, everybody,' I announce. 'Hats on!'

We make a pretty funny line-up here with all our hats on. Greysworth Bennett's lost property. I smile when I think about it. Home. I think we look a bit like a real life game of Guess Who? There's no guessing how this will go, but I feel stronger with these people by my side. Safety in numbers. Strength and solidarity in numbers.

Sue from Posers would be proud. This is all right up her street: civil disobedience, peaceful protest. I learnt from the master.

'Right, okay, everybody. Pencils and paper at the ready! Let's do this!'

The great thing about this is at first there's really nothing unusual or untoward to see. We just look like a group of art students (which, *hello*, is the look I've been going for ever since I can remember!). The plan is that when we start installing our work in the gallery and stick it onto the walls, that's when we attract attention.

Speaking of drawing attention, I glance over at Blaine who appears to be drawing a self-portrait. Wow, that boy is so self-centred. Is there any situation he can't make all about him?

Imagine being in a museum filled to the rafters with some of the finest works of art in the world and deciding you're the most interesting thing to draw a study of!

OMG, self-portraits are just pre-camera phone selfies, though, aren't they? I wonder if Van Gogh got a load of crap for being shallow enough to paint himself and exhibit it. I wonder if Rembrandt hated having his portrait painted unless it was by himself.

It doesn't take long to find a pair of breasts to draw. I'm sketching a scene from a famous Manet oil painting called *Le Déjeuner sur l'herbe*. It means 'Lunch on the grass', and it depicts a woman having a picnic in the buff, nude-butt naked, with a couple of fully clothed men. Sitting on grass with bare legs and a skirt is bad enough, so eating something as crumbly as a baguette in a forest without any knickers would just be the most uncomfortable thing ever.

There are actual reporters and photographers here; this means they've heard about us. This is great. This can be our way of controlling the narrative.

'This thing is so hot!' Audrey pulls her red balaclava over her sweaty face and her hair frizzes out like a flip-book animation of every imaginary hairstyle I've ever pictured on Tom's head.

Okay . . . we've had a bit of time to make drawings and

paintings and poems. I look round at my gang and we give each other the nod.

I tack my drawing onto one of the walls and everyone else is doing the same.

'Paige, come here!' Audrey waves me over to help with the women who are unfurling the banner. It says STOP LOOKING AT MY TITS in tall hand-quilted letters. YES! We pose for the photos, holding pens and pencils in the air and smiling.

Paul and Johnny shimmy and shake their T-shirts, and it is a beautiful sight to behold.

Some gallery visitors applaud us. Some just look at us like we're mad. But they're looking, that's the main thing.

Before long men and women with radios descend on us, waving their hands for us to stop, pulling our sketches off the walls.

This goes on until we're forcibly moved by security. Two guards are on either side of me holding my arms and legs. I haven't been in a position this compromising since winning the wheelbarrow race with Alison McGee at sports day in Year Six.

Result!

OH NO YOU POMPIDO-N'T

Next on our itinerary is the Pompidou. I can see how I went wrong trying to find this place the other day. I must have turned off the Rue de *Something* too early and wandered into the doll museum. As our art mob passes by the Poupée gates, I spare a thought for the doll doctor, who is no doubt working away on her plastic patients in there right now.

'This is it.' The Pompidou Centre reflects in Audrey's vintage sunglasses.

From outside it kind of looks like it could be related to Noo-noo from the Teletubbies. It's all made of exposed pipes and tubes. It looks like a big industrial hoover. You wouldn't necessarily assume that the largest collection of modern and contemporary art in all of Europe is squashed inside it, not unless you'd marked that page of the guidebook like me!

We form a little circle in the square in front of the gallery entrance. Pep talk time.

'Okay, everybody, so we got a good reaction at the Musée d'Orsay – well done, you were all great! If you've just joined us from that museum, then, first of all, hi and thank you, and, secondly, what is most important is that when we go into the Pompidou we don't want to attract attention from security and staff . . .'

I look round the huddle of faces, eager eyes hanging on my every word like I'm a gum-chewing football manager and just a second half away from winning the World Cup.

'We need to get in there and look as casual as poss. Make sure you're watching each other, find an area to draw in and once you see somebody else Blu-Tack their work on the wall, then you can do the same. That's when the real protesting begins. Sing, dance, perform, strike a pose – BE SEEN.'

I notice a bloke with a professional-looking paparazzi-style camera. He's followed us here and that's good. I'd rather he was snapping pics of us instead of crawling around in gutters, hoping some poor reality star will accidentally flash her knickers on the way out of a cab.

'You're more than welcome to photograph this, please just wait for the "flash mobbing" to take place so that you don't give us away too early.'

'*Bon.*' He nods his head, and chews his real-life gum as if he's trying to compete with my imaginary football manager mastication.

'Is there anything I'm forgetting?' I ask Audrey with all the answers.

'Remember to have fun!' She smiles with her red balaclava pulled back over her ears, framing her wolfy face perfectly.

'Before we get kicked out of here, Paige, you should really see the views of the city from the top floor,' Johnny suggests.

We all get on the escalator up to the top of the building to have a look at the views of the city. It moves at a slow, snaily pace, which does nothing for my adrenaline. Even that bloke with the camera comes along for the ride and he looks like he's getting impatient. But, oh, from all the way up here Paris is so beautiful that I can almost hear my heart break.

'You're a force to be reckoned with. Attagirl!' Mademoiselle Gigi pats me on the shoulders and lights a cigarette up on the viewing platform.

I can't fully enjoy the sweetness of her trying to big me up here on top of the most perfect beautiful city, like we're the glacé cherry plopped upon a big dollop of cream, because I can't fully relax with her breaking the rules. In this way. Right before we . . . break the rules of the gallery.

'Gigi, *pardon*, but I don't think smoking is allowed up here,' I explain, hissing because I don't want us to get told off. Not yet anyway.

'That young man of yours will get us all into trouble.' She rattles with laughter, motioning at Blaine, who also appears to be taking this op to roll a cigarette.

I march over to him, pinching the rollie out of his fingers and throwing it over the edge of the viewing terrace. '*Not now, Bernard!*'

Don't ask me why that came out of my gob, but it did. If only a big purple monster would come and gobble Blaine up. That would probably make this task a lot easier. There's no way we could ignore him like everybody ignores Bernard unfortunately. If there's one thing Blaine is yet to master, it's the art of subtlety.

Mademoiselle Gigi must sense the sheer lunacy in my eyes because she stubs out her fag without hesitation. 'The only person I do that for! I choose you over cigarettes, Tumbleweed!'

'*Merci, mademoiselle*,' I giggle, thinking *Thank God* inside.

We take a minute to limber up, sharpen our pencils

and exercise our vocal cords, before going down into the main gallery.

Our mob meanders through the bright white space. I'm careful not to talk to anyone at this point. I stay close to the gang, but I want to concentrate on the paintings on the wall. There are things I've only seen in books or in IKEA frames. Pollock. Rothko. Kandinsky.

I'm having a great time eavesdropping on a convo between the couple of art flash mobbers who are carrying the rolled-up banner. Hearing them speak is like tuning into a podcast.

'Of course, Picasso's work *stinks* of misogyny!' one of them says to her friend who nods in stoic agreement.

Really? I had no idea until now. Okay, I must find a book about this when we get back to Pages of Paris. I need to do some further reading. Why hasn't Mr Parker taught us anything about that in art?! Why, instead, does he insist on spending an entire term drawing still-life composition in the Cubist style of Picasso?!

I cannot wait to go to uni so I can actually ask all these big stonker questions and get some straight answers from lecturers who know their stuff, rather than a blank look from Mr Parker who's too busy telling us we'll never get a place on our first-choice courses.

All right. Audrey just winked at me. That's the signal. Like synchronised swimmers, the lot of us start flipping sketchbooks open, dipping nibs into inkpots, drawing and scribbling away and the silent concentration falls over us all.

It feels like the quiet before the storm. We are the swollen grey clouds, fit to burst and pour at any moment.

Gigi is the first person to tack her drawing on the wall this time. What she's made looks incredible. The rest of us begin to follow suit. We sing and dance and chant. We're really doing it. Taking shared ownership of the space, much like Pages of Paris.

Family visitors watch and children join in, singing and scribbling with crayons and clapping their chubby little hands together. It's a party!

The staff here are more chill than they have been at the other galleries. The attendants stand back in a line and watch us get on with it. It's like they've already heard about us, and are *sort of* treating this like it's a piece of performance art.

It's not long before security arrive and I feel a firm tap on my shoulder. Everybody out. Disruption accomplished.

THE SCENE
OF THE CRIME

We are swept along by the sea of tourists at the Louvre.

'This is why nobody likes this place,' Audrey grumbles in my ear.

'You know Beyoncé and Jay-Z had the whole gallery to themselves, right? That's the only way you could ever get an Insta-worthy selfie with our *Mona*.' Paul shakes his head as somebody stops still right in front of him as they fiddle about with their audio-description app thing.

'It's okay, you lot, this is good. We want a crowd. We want everyone to see us!' I do my best to convince them that coming here at peak time is the best idea.

This feels very different to the last time I was here. For a start I'm LOVING the busy corridors; I'm not bothered about Blaine finding somewhere quiet for us to hide. He's skulking around at the back of our party somewhere. I'm up front.

We need to blend in. If one of the guards from last time spots us, then they could stop this from happening before we've even begun. I have purposely shoved my beret into my pinafore pocket for this reason. The hat only goes on when the protest kicks off.

We enter one of the main rooms; yes, this is the one. *Liberty Leading the People* by Eugène Delacroix hangs on the wall. Crowds of visitors clamber for a good view, craning their heads to take in the enormous scale of her.

All right, Lib. Nice to see you again. Glad you're keeping well.

This is it. I open my sketchbook and draw Liberty and her flag.

Liberté, égalité, fraternité. Liberty. Equality. Fraternity.

Can women in art be really considered equal to men if the only times they make an appearance on the walls they've got at least one boob on show?

'WATCH IT!' a voice hollers over the hum of people in the room.

It's Blaine. What the hell is he doing?!

'These were actually really expensive shoes,' he informs a member of the public who has accidentally trodden on his toe. 'I mean, yeah, I was gifted them, but that's really not the point.'

His voice is so loud! This is not part of the plan. What an arrogant, ignorant hypocrite!

I am fuming. I dart across the room. I need to tell him to be quiet. We need to blend in until we reveal our real intentions for the protest!

'Blaine, be quiet, you're going to ruin this for everyone!' I stop dead still when I see the security guard – THE ONE WHO KICKED US OUT BEFORE – approach to see what all the fuss is about.

The guard sees me and I see the look of recognition and disbelief on his face.

Crap!

'*Non, non, non! Arrêtez-vous!*' He points and runs to get backup from the other guards.

We have to act fast to make this work.

'Art mob, assemble!' It's all I can think to shout and it works, the banner flies up in front of Lady Liberty, the camera shutters flash and we sing and chant and hold our artworks in the air. Just as they did before, tourists stand around to watch us, phones record us and upload us onto social media. Tweets are tweeted, more feet are trampled on, babies cry, disruption and chaos ensue.

Gigi refuses to budge when the guards with big guns try to pull her away. I'm worried for a second before remembering what a badass she is.

'Bring it on!' she sings.

Audrey looks fierce (and quite hot and sweaty) in her red ensemble. Lots of people are taking photos of her as she stands on the velvet bench, spiral-bound sketchbook held open with the words *THIS IS ART* scrawled in thick black Sharpie marker pen.

I am so proud of us all. I am so proud to be part of this group. It's like the Bennett's occupation all over again. Though yet again, Blaine has nearly put his (apparently very expensive) foot in it.

LIKE
NEW YEAR'S EVE
BUT NOT

There's no way I could go back to Greysworth without seeing the Eiffel Tower in real life. To celebrate our gallery protests our art mob has trudged to Paris's most iconic landmark. Surprise, surprise, Mademoiselle Gigi has another box of wine in her shopping trolley. We crowd around her as she perches on a bench under the tower and fills our water bottles with dark, vinegary *vin*. This is surreal. Just an hour ago, we were giving our details to police after being dragged out of the Louvre. Obviously that was pretty nerve-racking, but I followed Gigi's lead. She was so cool about it and Audrey told me that what Gigi was saying was along the lines of 'If you need to ask my name, then you've been living under a rock all your life.'

Now we're looking up at the Eiffel Tower, waiting for its lights to switch on and twinkle in the night sky.

Imagine giving it all the talk about not buying anything or contributing to capitalism one minute and then throwing a strop when someone accidentally steps on your designer shoes. It doesn't matter how well that went in the end – I am still so mad at Blaine. I can't really believe he has the audacity to be here; he nearly blew it for everyone.

Our cheeks are rosy in the cold night air. There are blokes selling those plastic spinny glowstick things. Couples getting engaged. French teenagers getting boozed up.

'Promise you'll stay in touch, Paige. One day, I wish to visit Greysworth! You must show me where you're from.' Audrey must be high on life, or this wine is much stronger than Gigi's letting on.

'Wow, if you really want to. I don't think you know what you're letting yourself in for,' I say, wincing.

I have a feeling she might change her mind when she hears from her poor unfortunate colleagues who have been stranded in Greysworth while we've been living it up here.

'What are you doing here, Blaine?' I hiss. 'Aren't you worried that your EXPENSIVE shoes might get muddy in the park?'

'What's your problem, Paige? Can you not just give it a rest? Everyone's having a good time; don't bring down the mood.'

'What's my *problem*?!' I blink at him. 'You are my problem! Oh my God, you're the worst! Could you really not stand to miss an opportunity to make something all about yourself?'

'That's rich coming from you, isn't it? *Oh yeah*, you're such a goody-goody!'

'Excuse me? Did you just say goody-goody?' I know I'm squawking instead of talking. 'Are you twelve? That would make perfect sense actually.'

He turns to walk away from me but I'm only just getting started so I go after him.

'I wouldn't expect you to understand. When was the last time you did something for someone else? You're as privileged and spoilt as they come. Thinking that if you talk the talk, then no one will notice that you're just a brat who needs his dad to get him a job.'

It's the countdown to when they turn on the twinkly lights. Everybody is shouting, '*Dix! Neuf! Huit! Sept! Six!*'

It's like it's New Year's Eve, but obvs it's not, otherwise I'd be watching Jools Holland, three Cadbury selection boxes deep, instead of dealing with this absolute pain in the arse, loves-himself, pretentious posh boy pretending he's a tortured artist, who must wear shoes more battered than Oliver Twist's nobody's-looking loungewear!

'You're very quick to judge me, Paige. But you're not so perfect yourself. I know you cheated on the Paris hat draw.'

I gasp, like I actually gasp in such a dramatic manner that I shock myself. I have to turn round to check if that gasp came from me or if there's a gasping-sound-effects pro stood right behind me.

'What? How? How could you possibly know that?'

'I heard you telling Holly about it. You thought I couldn't hear you because you were whispering in the Transport section and no one ever goes there, but, oh my God, you whisper louder than anyone I've ever met before.'

'*Cinq! Quatre! Trois! Deux!*'

He IS a mole! Maybe Bennett's Maxine was right all along. She and Bruce suspected that his head office dad had planted him in Greysworth to spy on us.

'Loud Whispering. You should put *that* in your personal statement. You're a *pro* when it comes to that.'

The tower dazzles in the night's sky. It looks like a really gloriously tacky Christmas tree decoration. It's breathtaking. We both freeze and watch it glow until it stops.

'I can't believe you said that. Knobhead.'

'You know what, forget it. Let's just end it here.' He shakes his head.

End what?

'I don't want anything more to do with you, Paige. Leave me alone.'

NEWS FROM NOWHERE

My phone pings. It's a video. I hold it under the counter to open and play it.

I know there's no Tony on patrol to tell me to put my phone in my locker here at Pages of Paris. I've seen the others working here text in front of customers and it's totally fine. In fact, maybe I'll record that happening and send it to Tony as an example of 'It's really not the end of the world, so get over it'.

But still, old habits die hard. If it wasn't for years of texting secretly inside the pages of the AQA poetry anthology at school, then maybe I wouldn't feel like such a criminal doing it at work.

I press play. It's a TV screen. I can just about make that out, but I can barely hear what the reporter's saying, even when I hold the speaker right next to my ear, but images of our 'demo' at the d'Orsay flash on screen before showing that original Louvre CCTV beret shot of me again. Tiny voiceover from the news reporter, '*Sources believe that these protests are linked to an incident at Paris's most famous art gallery just days ago . . .*'

'WHAAAAAAT!!! PAIGE!!!'

It's Holly's face. Up close. This is normal; she sends up-close vids of herself to me all the time. Sometimes she's lying on her back with the camera at a deliberately unflattering angle, while she sings along to the radio with salt and vinegar Pringles in her mouth doing the duck-beak thing. This time she's just talking, so I adjust the volume on my phone.

'Paige, OhMyGod, I don't believe this! I'm just in the Bridge Cafe getting cheesy chips for lunch and LOOK! I cannot believe this!'

The camera spins, and the beige interior of our fave Greysworth greasy spoon flashes by. Then it lands on the bloke in the apron, stood with one hand on his hip, the other pointing a remote at the wall-mounted telly. He's waiting for Holly to give him the go-ahead. 'Are you ready, my love?' he says, glasses on a necklace resting on his large pinny-clad chest.

'Yes please, Mickey! Press play!' Holly's voice is off camera. 'Paige! Is that YOU?! On the NEWS?!'

The camera zooms in on the telly and I can't really hear what it's saying, but, yep, sure as anything, that's MY HEAD on the CCTV at the Louvre yesterday.

'This is amazing, Paige! Tell me everything!'

COVER BLOWN

The drawing flash mobs have gone viral and attracted a lot of attention online. Luckily the reaction has been much more positive than the original Louvre drama. And I'm so proud that it seems to have drawn a lot of attention to Pages of Paris.

A photo of the sign in the window about the drawing protest got retweeted thousands of times and people all over the world have been sending messages of support and solidarity, telling stories about their memories of being Tumbleweeds here. It's gorgeous.

I've been speaking to Johnny about putting an exhibition of our gallery sketches together and hanging it in the shop and the cafe. He's really keen on the idea and thinks we should get it going *tout de suite*.

Audrey scrolls though emails at the computer behind

the bookshop till. 'Wow, Mademoiselle Gigi won't believe her eyes! Our inbox is full of people asking if they can come along to the life-drawing classes.'

A video of Gigi saying 'Bring It On' at the Louvre has been made into a GIF. Iconic.

'That's great! You'll defo need a life model with stronger stamina for that. No offence, Victor.'

I think about how Gigi might need a bigger trolley to fit all the extra booze. She'll manage, I'm sure.

'This person even says she wants to come here for our life-drawing class because she's heard so much about the flash mob gallery occupations!'

Somebody in the shop actually just asked for my autograph. That's mental. *I've* never even asked anyone for an autograph and I'm a huge fangirl. When Holly was really small her dad took her to Wickes for some meet and greet with a bloke called Handy Andy who used to be on some telly home-makeover show. Apparently he was too embarrassed that the signed piece of MDF was for him so he got Holly to ask. Even though I filled Hello Kitty notebooks with fake grown-up signatures when I was eleven, the graft that I put in then really didn't help me at all today. I was so freaked out I could barely spell my own name.

'You're famous! Oh my God! *Mon Dieu!* Is that Paige Turner from England?!' Audrey mocks me and I fall about laughing until a customer asks me to show them where the books on playwrights are.

'Follow me!' I say, leading the way through the chapters of the bookshop, ducking under shelves and winding through tunnels.

'Merci!'

'De rien!'

I skip back through the maze I've come to know like the back of my hand, grinning, the way that you only really do to yourself when you're having a genuinely great time, until I see Blaine and it wipes that smile right off my face.

We've been avoiding each other since we spoke at the Eiffel Tower last night. Mutually pretending that the other person doesn't exist, and it's been blissful.

But I catch him hunched over the old Pages of Paris typewriter. It's the *ping* sound that catches my attention. He's pulling at it, ribbon wrapped round the knuckles of his left hand, and his fingers are covered in ink! What is he doing to it?

I think about Johnny saying they could never get rid of it. I think of young Mademoiselle Gigi writing on it. No! It has a sign that says PLEASE DO NOT TOUCH!

I open my mouth to say something but I stop myself.

Whatever. I'm done with wasting my time on boys. Whether it's tortured-soul art-school boys, who are all dying to be the centre of attention, or seaside lads, who are never going to turn up on mopeds; they're just big whopping disappointments. I've got bigger, juicier, French fish to fry. I've got autographs to sign and books to read.

AN OFFER you CAN'T REFUSE

What better way to spend our last night in Paris than to invite all the new friends we've made over the past week for a bookshop party?

Audrey and I cart a load of crisps and cheese and bread and wine in bags from the supermarket. We're expecting a large turnout. A farewell and a gathering to celebrate the success of the gallery flash mobs.

When we get back to the bookshop that weird intense woman with the ever-changing glasses is here again. What does she want now? I'm not really in the mood for another staring competition.

She sits in the chair by the Pages of Paris typewriter. That's not an unusual thing to do; plenty of customers sit there, but they're usually reading something. She just looks like she's waiting. I don't know what she's waiting for; it's certainly not the Sunday-service bus to the big out-of-town Morrisons.

The little bald bloke in the suit is back too. He stands solemnly next to his scary-looking girlfriend. I could be totally wrong, I don't know her or what she's like when she's at home in her PJs watching the French equivalent of *Corrie*. All I'm saying is that if Simone were to jump up onto her lap for a stroke right now, she'd look like a classic bond villain.

'You're Paige Turner, aren't you?' She's really posh. English.

Am I in trouble again? Please, no. I know it's not a very rebel girl thing to think, but I'm too tired to be in trouble with anybody else.

'Allow me to introduce myself. My name is Claudine Bertaux, and I'm an art dealer.' She holds out a hand for me to shake. Rings on each finger.

'This is my assistant, Rodney.' *The assistant, of course.* He nods, while she does all the talking.

'I'm always on the lookout for fresh talent. The next big thing. You and your friends have certainly shaken things up.' She smiles at me from beneath her sharp fringe. Tonight she's wearing cat's-eye glasses with gold shiny frames. I was right – she must actually have her own personal branch of Specsavers.

'Thank you.' I say it carefully. Mostly because I really don't know where this is going.

'So, Paige, tell me, how do you think you might feel about selling your collection of sketches to one of Paris's top contemporary art galleries?'

I blink at her. 'Sorry . . . what are you talking about?'

'I'm interested in buying the girl in the hat sketches and exhibiting them. Giving them the showcase they deserve.'

'Really? Oh my God. I don't know what to say . . .'

'If you say yes, it will change your life.' Then Claudine smiles. She makes me feel like all three of the little pigs, but like she might blow my houses down with cannons of cash.

'Um . . . thank you, Claudine. I'm flattered.'

She pulls a business card out of her blazer pocket and asks Rodney to give her a pen before scribbling something down and passing it to me to look at.

'Here's my offer. If we shake on it here, then the money's yours and you'll get a say in how the work is installed. I understand you don't live in Paris, so we can arrange to fly you over here for the launch and for press opportunities. Mark my words, it'll be huge.'

'WOW.' I slap my hand over my mouth when I read the figure. I've never seen that much money in my life.

I feel like those people on *This Morning* who get a massive cheque delivered to their door by Peter Andre because they guessed that Madrid is the capital of Spain.

'Have a think about it and call me. My number is on the card.'

She's right. It *could* change my life. Imagine sticking THIS in my personal statement. If only Mr Parker could see me now.

And wow – if I got a place at uni, then this much money would make a ma-hoo-sive difference. I'd be able to afford tuition fees and rent. My mum wouldn't have to worry about it. And, oh my God, this would defo make up for the envelope of money I lost and the hard-earned Bennett's savings I've dipped into while I've been here.

Think of all the books this money could buy!

But.

But.

'But it's not just me,' I say. Claudine looks at me steadily. 'The sketches were a collective effort. I can't take all the credit. Me and my friends made this happen together.' I look around the shop, at all the books and the people who have become my friends in such a short, magical space of time.

Simone de Beauvoir the Cat slinks along the shelves

and starts meowing at me aggressively. She's joining in with the conversation. 'Come on then.' I lift her into my arms, a huge bundle of fluff, waaaaay heavier than I expected her to be, so that she can be at eye level with me and Claudine.

'I'm a Tumbleweed,' I explain, stroking Simone's head. Maybe *I'm* the Bond villain after all.

'I beg your pardon?'

'I'd love the girl in the hat sketches to be exhibited. That would actually be the coolest thing ever. I owe it to my friends. I owe it to this place. It's this shop that has brought us together. I want all the money to go here, to Pages of Paris. In the hope that it will stay here for another hundred years. In the hope that even more Tumbleweeds blow through this place and start their own revolutions.'

As I say that, I feel the bulb of a camera flash on the side of my face. It's not Blaine Henderson this time. I think I've just been papped again!

So it's official. I've evolved from Best Friend of Greysworth's Biggest Cultural Export, Paige Turner, into Your Number-One Stalker Fan. I'm collecting every single newspaper clipping with you in. I did start by sticking them up on my bedroom wall until my mum told me she'd take away my phone if I didn't put them in an album instead, because she didn't want to feel like she had a serial killer for a daughter. LOL! I'm so proud of you, Paige. I went into Smith's and told the boy working on the check-out that you're my best mate and that you're all over the news, all over Paris kicking elitist art-world butt! I cannot wait to see you soon so that you can teach me how to chat people up in French. And if you haven't learnt how to do that yet, then chop-chop! There's still time! Sending all my love from this beautiful picture of Lings Leisure Centre when it reopened in the late Eighties. Remember when I bashed my two front teeth out here at Andrew Butterworth's birthday disco party and you made sure I kept them safe in that Lion King party bag until your mum collected us? You'll always be my Bessie, Paige, even if you're a famous boob-freedom-fighting superstar! PS I think Sabine and Adam broke up today – the tension in the Military History section while they were picking returns was so thick you could have cut it with a knife. Updates and vegan sausage rolls when you're back XXX

My last night in my little squeaky Pages of Paris bed. I lie on my back, squinting at the phone screen. Mademoiselle Gigi miraculously produced another box of wine from her

pull-along trolley and we guzzled it to celebrate the fact
that we're the toast of the town! My thumbs slip on the
WhatsApp keyboard. Holly's online, I message her back.

Me: Holly, I wish you were here. This is mad. I have so
much to tell you.
Holly: Go on go on go on! I can't wait!
Me: Where do I begin? I've mastered the art of wearing
a beret! I've eaten THE BEST crème brûlée. I've made
friends with some really cool bookshop people and we
formed an anti-establishment guerrilla art movement and
we accidentally took the art world by storm. And we got
offered a LOAD OF DOSH that we'll use to keep Pages
of Paris, one of the city's most iconic bookshops, afloat
for the foreseeable future . . .
Holly: If that's not a personal statement, then I don't
know what is.

Hundreds of kiss-face emojis buzz through the screen.
I drop my phone on my face, smiling, and it whacks
me on the nose.

YOU CAN TAKE THE GIRL OUT OF GREYSWORTH...

This brand-spankin'-new Pages of Paris tote is, without a doubt, my favourite tote bag ever. I wear it into Greysworth town centre with pride. I think it makes me look worldly and intellectual.

I'm early for work, which is rare. Maybe I'm still on Parisian time. It's a late shift, so the shop's already open.

As I walk through the shop Adam is serving a customer at the till.

'*Bonjour, Mademoiselle Turner*!' he calls out. 'I cannot wait to hear all about your trip with lover boy!'

'Ughhhh!' I roll my eyes and Adam remembers he's supposed to be serving the customer at the till. 'Sorry, sir, if you'd like to enter your pin . . .'

I head up to the staffroom. Empty. Smells like microwave ready meals and coffee. It's good to be back. No sign of

Holly and she's due on the same shift as me. I can count the times I've beaten her to work on one hand. Because I think it's only happened once. I can't wait to unload my Parisian souvenirs on her! I have a stripy paper bag filled with quality hand-picked tat. I take out a pen and write 'For Holly x S.W.A.L.K. x' That stands for Sealed With A Loving Kiss. When we were in Year Five her older cousin, Kerry, had a caravan holiday romance with a boy called Jessie, and his parting gift was a love note that we were allowed to look at but not touch. This is when we learnt about SWALK and at times like this I think it still comes in handy.

After carefully examining the plates in the cupboard above the sink and finding one that'll be clean enough to do the job, I arrange the little cakes I brought back for everyone and leave them on the table ready to be gobbled.

What's this?

A brown envelope with my name on it.

For Paige.

B x

I know this writing.

I open it carefully and find a stack of black-and-white photographs.

Paris. The art nouveau Metro signs. The dusty, wonky

stairs in the bookshop. Mademoiselle Gigi necking a cup of red wine, between giving instructions during life drawing. Ugh. The photo I hated Blaine for taking when we were on the Eurostar on our way out. Blurred, out of focus. Here's a picture he's taken in an old junk shop. You can just make out his reflection in the old gilt-edged mirror. That boy is so vain. There's a snap of Audrey looking mischievous on the night of the gig, her dark eyebrows arched like a sexy tuff chick pixie on a beer-soaked toadstool. Simone in all her fluffy glory, stretched out on her back across a very old edition of *The Complete Works of Shakespeare*. Some of these photos have turned out all blotchy and out of focus. I think this one was taken at the Eiffel Tower but it's kind of hard to tell.

No offence but I reckon some of the pics I took on my phone are waaaay better than this. It just goes to show a fancy camera isn't everything. Money can't buy you talent.

Then there's a picture of me. I didn't know this was being taken. It was on the day we went to the Musée d'Orsay. I'm looking at a bookstall on the Left Bank. It's funny, I rarely like pictures of me that other people have taken (especially if I'm on the run in a hat that didn't really do anything for me) but this one has serious profile-pic potential. I look . . . I like how I look. Happy. I'm in Paris, with books and the sun shining on me.

The staffroom door swings open behind me and I shove the photos back inside the envelope. I *cannot* be seen gawping at a portrait of myself!

It's him.

'What d'you think?' he asks, leaning on the counter of the kitchenette. He flicks the kettle on to boil.

'Yeah. They're nice, um . . . You didn't have to.' Really, he did *not* have to. My camera roll is packed with snaps from that trip. Just because I don't have some fancy film camera that boys like him will bid serious dosh for on eBay doesn't mean I can't take my own photos.

'I just wanted to say sorry. I know how much that trip meant to you,' he offers.

'You wanted to say sorry by giving me a load of pictures *you* took? Including one of me looking like an actual swamp creature on the Eurostar . . . ? Cool.' I'm being difficult, but I don't care. He's not my friend. We didn't choose to go on a holiday together. It wasn't all Lads On Tour, matching T-shirts for Paige and Blaine's Mad Baguette Bender Weekender. I only sat next to him on that train because I had no other choice.

We didn't travel back together. I assumed he was

avoiding me after our exchange at the Eiffel Tower, but I really didn't mind. It actually worked out quite well; I spread out across both seats and finished the final chapter of *The Woman Destroyed*.

Anyway, how could he have any idea about how much anything means to me? He's so selfish, he hasn't got a clue.

'Did you read the other thing inside the envelope?' He points a teaspoon in the direction of the envelope.

What's he on about? I make sure that I don't look excited. I don't want to look excited by anything that boy does. I'm not falling for it.

I pull the photographs back out of the envelope and try not to get any greasy fingerprints on them.

There's something else inside. A folded piece of paper, so brown and old it looks like somebody's tea-stained it and singed the edges with a lighter for a history project.

I read it and he watches me from the other side of the room.

At first it doesn't make any sense, so I go over it a couple of times. Mechanical, typewritten words in French and the name Gigi Flambé.

The only sound in the room is the whirring of the kettle.

'Oh my God. Blaine?'

I hold the piece of paper up to the light, examining

it like I'm one of the experts on *Antiques Roadshow*.

'I found it. Gigi's Pages of Paris diary entry.'

'How? Where did you get this?'

'I just had a proper root through that office. At first I wasn't sure if it was the right one, because I'm not great at French and I had no idea Gigi's last name was Flambé . . .'

'Me neither!' I shake my head in disbelief.

'I know, right! So I checked with her and asked if you could have it. She said I could take it away on one condition . . .'

'OMG, what did she make you do?'

'She said it was all yours if I fixed the typewriter before I left.'

I think of him hunched over the old machine covered in ink. That's what he was doing.

'I can't even read what it says, but according to Johnny it's just a list of "fabulous qualities" Gigi felt she possessed at the time. She wrote it when she was young and hanging around with Margot.'

'No way!'

'I think some of them are pretty X-rated, but I didn't ask her to go into detail.' He chuckles.

'I can't believe this, Blaine . . .'

'I suppose in some ways this is Mademoiselle Gigi's

personal statement . . . from the days long before UCAS and student finance . . .' he says. 'And I know you'll think I'm being an entitled prick for even saying this, because I know you think I don't get the whole personal statement thing and, TBH, I don't really. But one of the best things about you is that you call me out on my prickery.' He laughs. 'You're not afraid to say what you think.'

'Did you just say "*TBH*"?' I grin.

'Don't look at me like that; it's obvs a bad habit I've picked up from you.'

All of sudden I realise how close we're standing to each other. My face is just inches, no centimetres, no millimetres – I don't know, metrics have never been my strong point – away from my face.

Is this? Are we?

SEALED
WITH a LOVING KISS

Are we actually really kissing? In the staffroom? His lips are on mine. Mine are right back on his. We both hold it there for a matter of seconds. In this room. The staffroom. Land of the boring start-up meetings and reheated microwave chilli.

Really?!

My eyes are wide open. I'm staring right at him, but this is a plot twist I did not see coming.

Kissing Blaine feels weird. Like wearing tights with no knickers or eating the furry skin off a kiwi or stroking a cat's fur in the wrong direction.

Holly swings into the staffroom, greasy paper bag in hand, and everything is happening so fast. 'YOU CAN TAKE THE GIRL OUT OF GREGGS, BUT YOU CANNOT TAKE THE GREGGS OUT OF THE – WHOA!!!

OH GOD! NO WAY! OKAY!'

'No! Holly! It's not what it looks like –'

She's out of that door faster than I can say 'Cheese and onion pasty and a Chelsea bun please'.

Blaine is still here, and so am I.

'If it's not what it looks like . . . then what is it?' he asks, grimacing a bit.

'Blaine, I . . . I think that felt really weird and wrong.'

'Oh my God, me too!' He breathes a (possibly much too strong) sigh of relief.

'Yeah?'

'Totally.'

'It was like . . . realising you've got dressed and left the house without putting any deodorant on. Just feels off. I don't feel "that way" about you.'

He laughs. The laugh dimple is out on the town. 'I don't feel it either. Because we're mates. Right? I hope we can be mates?'

'I hope we can be mates,' I say, smiling. 'I mean, you're a Bookshop Boy now. We have to at least try to get along.'

He chuckles. 'We'll always have Paris!'

'That much is true!'

Tony shuffles through the door. 'Oh, of course. You two are back.' Without even looking up to make eye contact or ask us how it went he plonks himself down on a chair and shoves one of my French cakes in his gob. Classic. It's good to be back. Everything is as it should be. The planets have realigned.

'Is it safe to come in now?' Holly pokes her head into the room. 'Your pasty's getting cold, Paige!'

'You are an angel. Y'know I've really missed these,' I say, clutching the bag in my hands. 'Nearly as much as I've missed you.'

'We have A LOT to catch up on, Mademoiselle Turner . . .' She wiggles her eyebrows at Blaine and I hush her up.

'Wow.' She grabs my arm and holds my wrist to her nose, sniffing hard. 'You even *smell* Parisian!'

'On my way back through the Eurostar terminal I shoved a load of those little paper perfume sample sticks in my bag . . .' I explain, sniffing my own skin. 'I didn't have enough money to buy an actual bottle but I'm glad the smell has clung to me.'

'Okay then, I'll crack on with the start-up meeting.' Tony adjusts his specs and reads the scrap of paper in his hand about yesterday's takings. 'We're down on target, as you'd expect at this time of year . . .'

As he talks facts 'n' figs I notice the Rubber of Destiny is lying on the coffee table. What's it doing up here?

Somebody's removed it from its natural till-point habitat. Will it lose its accuracy if used in the staffroom I wonder? I hold it tightly in my fist. Close my eyes and ask it a question with all the concentration and secrecy of a birthday-cake-candle wish.

FLIP.

Oooh. Look at that. What do you know? It actually says YES.

FIN

ART GALLERY BINGO

Next time you're in an art gallery, whether or not you're starting a revolution like Paige, see if you can spot these things. If you get a full house, then you deserve to go on a wild spending spree on postcards in the gift shop (that's the best bit of any gallery or museum anyway, right?).

A gift shop	Angsty art students sketching	Boobs in a painting
Somebody taking selfies	A cherub	Old ladies
Anything made by a female artist	An insta-worthy self portrait	An amorous couple on a romantic break for two

VINTAGE HEAVEN

Picture yourself in one of Paris's coolest vintage shops with Paige. What would you take back to Greysworth in your suitcase? A groovy sixties mini dress? A pair of cute cat-eye shades? How about a big froofy wedding gown for your next shift at Bennett's?

Acknowledgements

My mum brought up me and my little brother to write those thank-you cards to everyone who came to our birthday parties. After all of the crispy cakes had been scoffed, the balloons had gone all wrinkly and the vouchers had been spent on cool new CDs/make-up/Beanie Babies, I'd sit down to concentrate on saying thank you in my neatest handwriting.

Seeing my books on shelves has felt like all of my birthdays at once, so this is me saying thank you to the people who helped to make it happen. Just imagine that this is written in multicoloured gel pens on Hello Kitty-branded note cards and that it smells like just blown-out and wished-on candles.

Dear Fliss, thank you for reading my Bookshop Girl manuscript and turning it into a real book, and then a real thrillogy! Thank you for stretching me to write seaside AND Parisian adventures for Paige.

Dear Jenny and Alex at Hot Key, thank you for putting all of the pieces of Bookshop Girls One, Two and Three together to make them Top Stunners!

Dear Polly, thank you for taking me and Paige on, and for talking us up, showing us to the world.

Dear Darling Gorgeous Friends, thank you for all of your support behind the scenes of Bookshop Girl. Thanks for being constant inspos to me and putting up with all the times I make notes of funny things you say as they happen.

Thank you to all of the Bookshop Babes who have recommended my books to readers, and to the bloggers and librarians who have said great things about Paige and Holly.

Dear Joe, thank you for being a real-life cherub, for being with me the moment this book fell into place, and for making all of the other moments you're with me feel like a birthday party.

Dear Oscar, thank you for being the best little brother, for showing me how to eat Viscount biscuits layer by layer and for hauling *Bookshop Girl* all the way to China with you.

Thank you, Dad, for being so proud of these books and inventing the Touch the Book game in the first place.

Dear Mum, thank you for all of the holidays you gave us when it was difficult to have holidays, and thank you for making a hotel room baguette picnic a treat.

I'd like to say thank you to my grandma and grandpa, who we lost while I was writing this book, for all of the stories they told us. Stories that spanned continents and decades and lifetimes. I hope they're stocking *Bookshop Girl in Paris* in that big library in the sky.

Chloe Coles

Originally from Northampton, Chloe studied illustration at Cambridge School of Art before moving to London. Now in her twenties, she has worked in bookselling since the age of sixteen, squeezing it in around school and university and other jobs. She's previously worked at Waterstones, Blackwells and Heffers and now works as a Children's Specialist and Assistant Buyer at Foyles Charing Cross. All of her hair is her own. People ask her about that. A lot. Chloe sings ('shouts') in a band with her best friend.

Follow Chloe Coles on Twitter @ChloeColes_